Janet Frame, New Zealand's most highly acclaimed author, was born in Dunedin in 1924 and died in 2004. Her first book, *The Lagoon and Other Stories*, was published in 1952. Frame went on to publish eleven novels, another three short-story collections and a book of poetry during her lifetime, and another novel, a short-story collection and a book of her poems have been published since her death. Janet Frame received numerous awards for her work, including a CBE for services to literature, in 1983. In 1990, she was made a Member of the Order of New Zealand. In that year, the three volumes of her autobiography were made into the film *An Angel at My Table*.

In 1973, Janet Frame was awarded the Katherine Mansfield Fellowship, and she spent the following year in Menton on the Côte d'Azur. Beneath the villa Isola Bella, where Mansfield lived and wrote for a time, is the Memorial Room, a small stone room commemorating her work and given to the Mansfield Fellow as a place to write.

Though she struggled to work in the difficult conditions of the Memorial Room—with no running water or toilet facilities and delays in receiving her fellowship payment—

it was in Menton that Janet Frame wrote *In the Memorial Room*, the story of Harry Gill, writer and recipient of the Watercress-Armstrong Fellowship.

Frame did not allow publication of the manuscript during her lifetime—would certain people see themselves in the characters portrayed and, finding unflattering portraits, be offended? But she always intended the novel to be published posthumously, at the right time. Tucked away, to be looked at later, the Menton novel waited while Frame went on to write *Living in the Maniototo*, a novel interlaced with some of the same characters, events and places.

Now, almost forty years after Janet Frame wrote *In the Memorial Room*, on her second-hand typewriter, the wait is over.

Janet Frame

In the Memorial Room

COUNTERPOINT
BERKELEY

With thanks to Hocken Collections—Uare Taoka o Hākena, University of Otago Library.
Extract from 'Little Gidding' (p.81) taken from *Four Quartets*, © Estate of T. S. Eliot, and reprinted by permission of Faber and Faber Ltd.

Cover design by W H Chong
Page design by Imogen Stubbs
Typeset by J & M Typesetting

Library of Congress Cataloging-in-Publication Data
Frame, Janet.
In the memorial room : a novel / Janet Frame.
pages cm
ISBN 978-1-61902-175-4 (hardback)
1. Authorship—Fiction. I. Title.
PR9639.3.F716 2013
823'.914—DC23
2013018057

COUNTERPOINT
1919 Fifth Street
Berkeley, CA 94710
www.counterpointpress.com

Printed in the United States of America
Distributed by Publishers Group West

10 9 8 7 6 5 4 3 2 1

IN THE MEMORIAL ROOM

Grateful thanks to the publishers
of Margaret Rose Hurndell for
permission to quote from her work.

Harry Gill's Menton Journal

Meeting and Invitation

September, 1973

Today I received word that my application for the Watercress-Armstrong Fellowship had been accepted and that I am to be next year's Fellow. The Committee would like me to visit Wellington for the presentation ceremony early in October, and I am to leave for France by a ship of the Paradise Line in early December.

Although I am not quite sure why I applied for the Fellowship I'm looking forward to travelling, although indeed I am not a traveller and my first voyage out to New Zealand when I was nine years old, in 1950, gave me enough experience, I felt, to last a lifetime. The money from the Fellowship, however, will give me a chance to write a different kind of novel from my first two which have given me the reputation of being an 'historical' novelist. *Wairau Days* might just be called an historical novel, but I did feel that *New Families*, with its emphasis on the private lives of the characters, might not have been dismissed as it was as 'another historical novel from the pen of a talented young writer'.

I'd rather like to write a comic novel in the picaresque tradition, a desire which is perhaps strongly proportionate to the lack of picaresque qualities in myself, for I am a dull personality, almost humdrum, a plodder from day to day with only an occasional glimpse of light, literally as well as figuratively for the disease in my eyes has worsened and in another three or five years I might not be fit enough to take up an overseas Fellowship: another reason, I suppose, why I applied for it. So here I am, shy, bespectacled, rather slow on the uptake, a reader and a student since my early childhood and an accidental novelist, for *Wairau Days* was written to correct or bring to full blossoming the half-truths of the story of Wairau. How surprised I was, that I so much enjoyed my task of telling the truth!

Although it has been a disappointment to my father whose natural desire was that I should qualify in medicine and take over his general practice, it alarms him less, now, that I should be on the way to being a successful writer (described as 'talented', and 'promising' and not yet too old to panic at the description) than that I should have continued my shilly-shallying of courses at university. The Entomological Course did interest me while I was studying it. And for a while the prospect of Ear-Nose-Throat held me spellbound, and my poor father's eyes were shining when he talked to his colleagues about me. Then came the blackout and the problem with my sight, and, though that seemed to be only temporary and the family accepted it as such and were cheered when by my accounts and those of the physician it improved (a physician is oblivious to his family's ills), I have not yet told them of the new problems with it. In some strange way I have fastened my hopes on the scholarship and Menton and I am determined to get there, and to enjoy it, and to write my new kind of novel, and then, when I return home, take whatever is waiting for me.

This last remark sounds schoolboyish, and might betray my English birth; it shows a recklessness which I have within me but which none may read in my face or behaviour.

I have a severe headache above my right eye.

~

October 3rd

The notice of the award appeared in this evening's newspaper:

WATERCRESS-ARMSTRONG FELLOWSHIP
TO YOUNG HISTORICAL NOVELIST

Harry Gill, 33, of Auckland, author of *Wairau Days* and *New Families*, has been awarded the Watercress-Armstrong Fellowship for 1974. He will leave at the end of November for Menton where he will live for six months working in one of the rooms of the Villa Florita, occupied during her lifetime by Margaret Rose Hurndell, the internationally known poet whose last three books were written at the Villa Florita before her death there in 1960. The Fellowship has been endowed as a living memorial to Margaret Rose Hurndell whose death at the age of thirty cut short a brilliant career.

So. Each of the five fellows before me has taken time to write a study of Margaret Rose Hurndell or to edit letters and one *actually discovered* an unpublished poem between the leaves of a book sold casually at the annual bazaar of the local English church. At the presentation ceremony in Wellington (which was held last week), when I was asked if I had any plans for making a study of Rose Hurndell I replied that I did not know, I would see how the land lay at Menton, although inevitably Rose Hurndell would be in my thoughts.

I said I admired some of her poems very much, particularly those of the last book, *Rehearsals*.

Two ladies at the presentation (there seemed to be mostly ladies and very very tall men, almost with their heads near the roof, in the small group surrounding me), Connie Watercress and Grace Armstrong, the two principal donors of the Fellowship, replied that Rose Hurndell's first two books were their favourites, the ones written in New Zealand: *The Harbour*, and *Manuka Night*.

—Her poems have been translated into thirteen languages, Connie said. —And her *Letter to Procne* is now known all over the world. Just think!

I thought – just. There is such intense interest in Rose Hurndell's works, more so, naturally, now that she is dead, and her last poems have been compared in their purity and otherworldliness, their vision of death, to the Requiem music which Mozart left unfinished, and although they were written before her death they have the effect of being posthumous, of actually being written after death.

The conversation that evening was mostly about Margaret Rose Hurndell and her life and her family. I was told that her sister and her sister's husband had retired to live in Menton two years ago, and that two friends she had made when she lived in London came each year to spend the winter in Menton and to make a pilgrimage to the Villa Florita. Her work was known in the city. The city was proud that she had lived and died there – yes, they were even proud of her death there, although her body was taken to London to be buried.

Towards the close of that presentation evening, when suddenly the talk of Margaret Rose Hurndell had died away, someone asked me – I think it was Connie Watercress – what I planned to write in Menton. I said vaguely that I did not quite know.

—I'm afraid I haven't read your last book, Connie said. —But I've heard so much about it! *The New Family.*

I smiled and murmured, —Yes, *New Families.*

—There's a shortage of historical novelists in New Zealand, someone said, as if talking of petrol or transistor batteries or vacuum cleaners.

—So we're proud to have you.

—Will you be writing something historical, something French?

—Do you speak French?

—Did you know that Peter Cartwright, who's at Oxford now, thinks you are the finest historical novelist we've had? I haven't read your *Wairau Days* myself but he said it can't be faulted. I read an article about it in one of the English papers. I get the *Times* and *Guardian* flown over.

—The paper's too thin, airmail, don't you find? It tears.

—We're proud to have you. Perhaps there'll be more financial support for the Fellowship when they know you've got it. We have to advertise you a little, you know.

—He's blushing.

—So he is!

—Well, Harry, we'll soon get rid of those blushes.

—Your father's a doctor, I hear?

—

And so the conversation continued until one by one

the guests found their fur coats and went home, and I stayed a while by myself in the smoke-laden air, snaffling the last few savouries, for I was hungry, and a little drunk, and I went back to the hotel room where they'd booked me (I'd refused to stay with any members of the Committee who'd invited me) and I went straight to bed and fell asleep.

And I dreamed.

~

I dreamed.

I have definite views about a novelist's inclusion of dreams in his work. Dreams, I think, are for the first novel where all the material for the future is accumulated, packed tightly as in a storehouse the walls of which are strained to bursting point with their contents. Dreams may be inserted as extra provisions because the storehouse has no further room for solid material; dreams weigh nothing, do not need equipment for their transport and may have a chemical volatility which enables them to be replaced and changed often or annihilated when they are no longer of use. I maintain, however, they are one of the privileged tricks allowable only to the first novel, and, later, when the solid material has been withdrawn and used and the mind itself with the approach of middle and old age and death (not necessarily in that order) begins the process of confirming its doubt of the substantiality of the apparently 'real' world, as a preparation for its own final material dissolution, then dreams may re-enter the novelist's work: he may use them as he will.

This is just my opinion. I have been brought up with the disciplines of research and study with, perhaps, after observing my father at work since I was a child, a tendency to watch for symptoms, to diagnose a work of art, to determine the prognosis, the etiology, the epidemiology, and then to set about 'curing' it by writing it.

Therefore, after that preamble, I set down my dreams in what is a journal, not a novel.

~

That night, after the official presentation of the Watercress-Armstrong Fellowship, I dreamed I was back in my flat in Symonds Street, near Grafton Bridge, after visiting my parents at Northcote for dinner. I had just walked in the door when I noticed, sitting on the sofa that was rather worn and covered with a piece of Indian cotton I bought in Queen Street, a woman of about my own age or a few years younger, dressed in the rather short skirt of the late nineteen fifties, with a cashmere sweater, and – pearls, three rows, about her throat. Her hair was fair to gold, quite short and straight and she was slimly built and rather tall, with exceptionally large hands and feet which I thought ugly. She wore no makeup on her face which was rather too broad to be delicate or beautiful as one imagines beauty, but her eyes were the startling blue which is almost violet and so far known by me only inside fiction. She smiled at me. I had a feeling almost of horror when I realised that her perfectly formed white teeth were false – I could just discern the unnaturally pink plastic gums which have since been replaced in dental pros-thetics by a more natural colour. The colour of her gums dated, for me, the time of her acquiring her false teeth. She must have been twenty-two or -three then, if, as I guessed, she was now about twenty-nine.

—Well, aren't you going to say hello? she said.

Her voice was rather deep for her feminine appearance.

—Oh.

I felt myself blushing.

—Harry's blushing, she said.

—Oh. You must be Margaret Rose Hurndell?

—Rose Hurndell, please. The Margaret Rose is something I can't bear.

—I was nineteen when you died, I said.

She looked at me curiously.

—Did you know of me when I died?

—I didn't know your work, I said. —I knew *of* you, that you'd had a son and gone overseas and lived overseas. Someone showed me a book you'd written once. I didn't read it, I'm afraid. Studies and so on. And I've never cared for women poets with three names. I'm curious though. I hope you don't mind my asking but – when did you get your false teeth?

She laughed, showing more of them than I had seen before. The bright pink gums shone; they were horrible, I thought. A bright colour like carnations that have been painted for a flower show.

—I suppose you think it's rotten cheek my asking.

She laughed again.

—For God's sake don't sound like an English schoolboy. You *are* English, aren't you?

—I'm a New Zealander now.

—Well, for heaven's sake never use in my presence those awful dated words, ripping, bounder, jolly – you know. I got my teeth, by the way, on the National Health in London. Do you like them?

—They're ghastly.

—Don't use ghastly, either.

—Beastly, then.

—Nor beastly. Not rotten ripping bounder jolly chap. Where's your New Zealand speech?

—You're very fussy, I said, —for someone with such horrible teeth.

—They're even and white, are they not?

—Yes, but the gums, the gums!

—I know.

—The gums of Rose Hurndell.

~

It was an absurd dream. We simply sat there all evening exchanging absurd remarks. She didn't seem to me like a poet and I seemed to her like an English schoolboy out of a comic strip of the twenties. And that is all my dream, it simply drifted away. The next morning I took down from my bookshelf a copy of her

Fifty Living Men which I bought (the only one of her books I could find) when I knew of my scholarship award.

I read:

> The Ministerial prime
> a political summertime
> berg, baron, bedtime
> elective ice, infertile wives,
> an unfurnished room of nose-gays and lilies of the
> valley.

Not one of her good poems, I thought. All general, no particular. I read on:

> The general has slain
> has overcome the particular domain
> a man is men one is fifty fifty is one
> only there is no sun to be under
> time out of particular thunder
> the mind emerges kept honeyful and warm
> by a swarm.

I don't care for such poems. It occurred to me that in

another few years they'd be forgotten, that although Rose Hurndell had become well known and much read, one had only to look in the endpapers of old books to find the extravagant praises of forgotten authors. I fancied that seven or eight years is too brief a time after death for the kind of memorial which the Watercresses and the Armstrongs had founded, for their memorial gesture might find itself also engulfed in the gradual oblivion necessary before the re-emergence of those whose qualities of work survive decay. I suspected therefore that the founding of the scholarship was a means by which the Watercresses and the Armstrongs, denied fame in their journalistic endeavours, might snatch a little of its nourishing glory (as I had snatched the savouries after the ceremony, for I had been hungry, and all the rich invited guests had gone), sheltered and strengthened by the growth, blossoming and presence of Rose Hurndell as the small plants in the bush are sheltered and given life by the starry-blooming manuka. The title of Rose Hurndell's second book, *Manuka Night*, seemed appropriate in that setting.

I know, as I have said, that my own motives for applying for and accepting the scholarship are far from 'pure'. I am aware of the drama of 'the young man going blind'. When one is faced with such disasters in one's life one has to use the drama of the situation as a vehicle to go through it or bypass it. The name Menton has no particular appeal to me. I am curious of course about Rose Hurndell and her life and work. I shall be interested to meet her brother-in-law Dorset Foster and her sister Elizabeth who have travelled to set up their retirement home so far from their own country and who must have been lured by the fact that Elizabeth's sister lived and died there. No doubt I shall meet also the Louise Markham who left her husband Haniel and went to Menton to the Villa Florita to live with Rose Hurndell until her death. I have been told that both Haniel and Louise Markham have a permanent winter apartment in Menton. And the Watercresses who know Menton have told me, 'to put me in the picture' as they expressed it, of Liz and George Lee, the English couple who help to run the English library, of their own son Michael who, they say, is a promising writer. They have hinted that perhaps, who knows, when I arrive in Menton they will be waiting to welcome me and 'show me the ropes', a nautical term no doubt appropriate to use to one who sails in a few weeks to spend thirty-two days on board a ship of the Paradise Line.

~

My preliminary journal ends here. During my stay in
Menton I shall make notes in between writing a novel,
and when I return from Menton with (I hope) my
novel completed, I shall write the story of my tenure of
the Fellowship. Tenure is a word which appeals to me.

The Tenure

1

As one known purely as an historical novelist (the 'known' being an exaggeration as I believe a writer is not 'known' until his grocer and barber have read his works without astonishment) about to yield to the temptations of English fiction or, in the case of recording my experiences of the *tenure* of the Fellowship, English fact, I have an enticing range of possibilities beginning with *Beowulf*, *The Wanderer* and *The Seafarer* and continuing, as you are aware, through *Euphues*, Thomas More, Milton, and so on to Agatha Christie and Ian Fleming. Do you sense a slight lowering of standards towards the end? Is it the end?

How shall my story be expressed? How shall I bring myself alive to your ears and eyes, all your senses?

I have already described my face; you will have found nothing particular in it; you may have concluded that I am a mere particular in it; you may have concluded that I am a mere generality. The names of my two books, however, are definite, existing beyond me; you will certainly not have read them but you will have 'heard of' them or 'read of' them which is about all a young writer like myself can hope for and not be downcast by, unless, even when he is no longer young, the pseudo-reading of his work continues.

I have told you my age, and, vaguely, the course of my studies. I have mentioned my family, my origins. Unless you are to imagine that I am homosexual and unless I wish to encourage you in this belief because it is true, I must account for my personal relations between puberty and the present, and you may even wish me to explain to you why I have not yet married, for marriage today is an affair between schoolboys and schoolgirls and I, who have lingered, find myself questioned in a conforming society.

I haven't yet found anyone to love. There are people like me, you know, who are not given a large dose of libido and who conserve what they have for their own purpose of staying alive. The prospect of my blindness has, I'll admit, the effect of driving me at times into a state of panic and in such a state I may be likely to fall in love very quickly, at first sight, as one swallows a strong drink. I don't know. I would describe this present age as an age of Explanation when the overriding fear is that nothing should remain unexplained, and this, combined with the age of excess of literacy brings every man and woman to a state of watchfulness (Why did I do this? Why did I do that? Let me explain...) that is exceeded only by the watchfulness of nations and their elected or self-appointed guardians. The world has adopted the Boy Scout motto, 'Be Prepared', while remaining at the Boy Scout level of maturity.

My story, however, is of my *tenure* of the Watercress-Armstrong Fellowship. Like any young man setting out on a voyage I was filled with excitement and anticipation and (because of the problem with my eyesight which I did not speak of) there was at times an alarming fear that I was about to be struck 'the mortal blow'. Had I been ten or twenty years older I would not have dreamed of making this voyage, chiefly because by the time one reaches the forties and fifties the insulation against even the prospect of danger and disaster is wearing thin and the physical menaces of a walk from home to supermarket are now visible in detail and demand careful strategy, as if the likely victim were travelling thousands of miles to the other side of the world. I shan't describe my voyage on that famous ship of the Paradise Line that was overpopulated with anxiety-ridden immigrants returning with their families from the Pacific lands to their former dreamed-of homes in Holland, France, Germany, Great Britain with the intensity of the dream increasing the level of anxiety and the supposed 'permanence' of the move in a life where few things are permanent weighing so heavily on their minds and bodies that each morning the waiting room of the young bulbous-nosed arrogant doctor, who was scarcely more than a medical student, was filled to overflowing with sniffling, crying, groaning passenger-patients, while from the deckchairs ranged along the promenade deck came, from the would-be lotus eaters trapped thirty-two days in the ship of the Paradise Line:

> *a doleful song*
> *Steaming up, a lamentation and an ancient tale of*
> *wrong.*

The analogy with the lotus eaters was completed by the continuous playing of deck music,

There is sweet music here that softer falls.

No, I shan't describe that voyage, or my time spent day after day leaning over the deck-rail trying to get a voice or signal from the small transistor radio I bought, greedily, at duty-free prices; or lying in the tiny cream-painted cabin, trying to read in the dimmest light although all the cabin lights were switched on, almost driving myself to destroy my sight with word-trash instead of word-treasure, weighing the moral accept-ability of each form of destruction, and finding in the mutinous lunacy that seizes all passengers during that eleven-day journey, without land, across the Pacific, when one does not need to have killed an albatross to suffer the nightmare, that destruction by trash is more to be approved; and so I'll not describe my voyage which was filled with counterfeit words and phrases, eyes that followed around rooms, that dropped, glistened, drooped, glances that travelled and were exchanged and burned, hot looks that set the heart on fire, smouldering looks, hearts in ashes, ice-cold hearts and melting hearts. I wrote nothing. I read trash. I read one writer, however, who paid with his thought, paid exactly, for the use of his language. And yet of that I remember only the various uses that human beings may be put to – there was a man, the writer said, who lived in Edinburgh at the turn of last century and who rented his humped back in the streets as a desk for clerks to write their accounts upon.

My story, however, is of the *Tenure*. I disembarked from my ship of the Paradise Line (you will note my possessive pronoun after thirty-two days of sailing *within her*), and I travelled by train, not by *Le Train Bleu*, for I must tell you, as it is important in my story, that I am the kind of person who is inclined to miss the best trains, to find the worst rooms in hotels, the surliest waiters in restaurants; nor am I the kind of person to protest, for the life-long disability with my eyesight has accustomed me to the belief that others see the 'real' world but I do not – how can I when my eyesight is defective; I have to take the words of others and of the world on trust and be labelled variously with the same implication, a fool, a doormat, someone who is forever being imposed upon. I am the classic 'shy mild little man' who may resort to physical violence if he is desperate, or, if he is literary, to linguistic violence – well, there are many ways of facing the aggressor, if one can identify the aggressor. Someone once told me, however, that I am the uttermost fool, away at the end of the line, because I sometimes do not recognise that I am being imposed upon.

I travelled next to a seat I had reserved but it was already taken, therefore I did not argue. I sat up all night in an airless carriage, and I tried from time to time to perceive France, for this was my first visit anywhere 'overseas', but I saw reflected in the window only my own dust-distorted face and those of my five companions. I took out my French phrase book which I'd bought the week before my ship sailed (I studied French intermittently at school) and read most of the night, listening also to the conversation of my fellow passengers. From time to time I had a sensation of the greyness of the world which I supposed to be related to my eye condition, as if the rods or cones of my sight were being destroyed and I were to be left with the vision which they say cats have, of eternal greyness. Just before the train drew into Menton, in the early morning, I had been dozing, and I remember I wakened, and the green of the palms, the palms themselves, which made me think momentarily that I had travelled to the heart of a desert, they were so unlike trees I had seen anywhere before, seemed in their greenness to bathe my eyes with blessing – all the foliage of all the trees seemed to shine, as dew or rain had fallen.

I had wondered, before, whether in the process of losing my sight I would begin greedily to observe colour – or would it be shape and form – or the placing of the world, the composition of a room, a street, a view of mountains and the sea – would I begin to hoard the world, I wondered, as people hoard their possessions for the simple reason that they are dying and can take nothing with them? I did not even know the answer at the moment the train drew into Menton city. I felt, just then, a kind of indebtedness to green, as a colour. Do we possess most what we are indebted to? Could I have said, as a painter, or poet:

> Les Anges, sont-ils devenus discrets!
> Le mien à peine m'interroge.
> Que je lui rende au moins le reflet
> d'un email de Limoges.
>
> Et que mes rouges, mes verts, mes bleus,
> son oeil rond réjouissent.

S'il les trouve terrestres, tant mieux
pour un ciel en prémisses.

In that case one becomes what one is indebted to.

~

But my story is of the Tenure...

2

If you had expected me to tell you that Margaret Rose Hurndell, thirteen years dead, was on the station platform to meet me, you may be as disappointed as I would have been startled had it been so. I was, however, startled to find Connie and Max Watercress, whom I had last seen at the reception in Wellington, and a handsome richly bearded young man, the perfect stereotype of 'the young writer', whom they introduced as their son Michael, and his wife Grace, a tall large-boned fair-haired American with a sallow scar-pitted face and prominent teeth.

Naturally, they hurried to explain their presence. I realised that I was not mistaken in assessing the assessment of me by others – there had been some idea that I might not be able to cope (with my eyesight) with arrival in a foreign land, and so Connie and Max from New Zealand had arranged with Michael and Grace from England to be in Menton and welcome me *in force*, as it were.

—So here we are, Connie said, in rather self-conscious French.

—Welcome to Menton.

The four, chorusing the welcome, were joined by two other voices, one belonging to a smartly dressed eager-eyed and -faced woman in her fifties who gave her name as Liz Lee, Head of the Welcoming Committee, the other of her husband, George Lee, an Englishman in his middle sixties with an astonishingly unintelligible English voice which made him appear to be saying, through scarcely moving lips, then and whenever I spoke to him afterwards, one sentence only, *Angela will be livid*, from which one had to extract meaning and devise an intelligible appropriate answer, so that my conversation with him always went thus:

He: Angela will be livid.
I: Yes, I was there last week.

Or thus:

> He: Angela will be livid. Angela will be livid. Angela will be livid.
>
> I: I found it quite pleasant in its way, considering.

From time to time I had a dreadful thought that he might have suffered a stroke which made it difficult for him to move his lips in speech. My search to excuse will lead me always to the infirmities of mind and body; still, I'm not so much a saint that I did not enjoy the absurdity of our conversation and perhaps sense a hint of the power it gave him, of one who 'spoke with tongues', concealed amid the dreadful exposures of clear enunciation which were enacted around him.

After the welcoming ceremony at the station and the remarks that I must be tired, the six claimed my two suitcases for me, and saw me to a taxi, directing it to the Villa Paradiso where I had booked, by letter from New Zealand, for five days, choosing the Villa Paradiso out of the four suggested to me by Connie Watercress (Villas Maria, Rosa, Louise, Paradiso) with the wild extravagance of adventure which suggested that as I was travelling by a ship of the Paradise Line it might be just as well for me, on my arrival at Menton, to extend my stay in Paradise.

During my first three days at the Villa Paradiso I found a small one-room apartment which I could pay for with the rather meagre Fellowship and owing to the understanding of the patron of the Villa Paradiso I was allowed to leave after three days. So. There I was, three days in Menton, with a tiny sordid apartment to stay in, not far from the famous Margaret Rose Hurndell Memorial Room, which I had not yet seen, the key being held by one of the French officials of the town, and recovered enough from my journeys of the past five weeks to be ready for the official welcoming reception and dinner. These were held on my fifth day, in an order of creation, so to speak, and the reception, I'm told, though my memory was blurred by sea-travel and champagne, went very well, being held along with a reception for a retiring commander of the Navy, a native of Menton, so that most of the evening was devoted to naval speeches and conversations (with most of the guests sailors – in a way continuing the Paradise journey) while the speech to welcome me was delivered during one of the lulls which periodically occur in a cocktail party. Suddenly, I found the mayor advancing towards me, my name spoken aloud, photographers appearing and surrounding me, and Connie and Max and Michael Watercress and his wife Grace, and there was the gracious mayor extending his hand to – Michael Watercress. Of course. The stereotype author. I blushed miserably like a schoolboy. Apologetically the mayor turned to me and shook hands but the photographers had already taken their photos. An account of the ceremony appeared in *Nice-Matin* three days later, with a photograph captioned, *The Mayor shakes hands with this year's Watercress-Armstrong Fellow.* The photograph showed the gracious mayor extending his hand to Michael Watercress.

Standing near Michael Watercress, the perfectly presentable stereotype of the modern author, you could see if you looked closely, though half the body was out of the photo, a rather stocky young man with glasses and curly hair and a look of what might be frenzied embarrassment on his face. He was holding his hand in a mimicry of the bearded young writer's pose.

I must tell you that I was equally successful, or unsuccessful, at the dinner that evening, given at the famous seaside restaurant, where Michael Watercress – and why not? – mistaken for the Watercress-Armstrong

Fellow, was given three free bottles of champagne to take home. His protest was feeble; his delight was evident. I thought as I looked at him, *We're the same age.* Which is substance, which is shadow, and where, who, is the sun? I decided I would get to know him, his wife, and the Watercress family.

3

My apartment was a small room accommodating a double bed, an oil-cloth covered small table, an armchair and two wooden chairs and a large wardrobe with a drawer and a door-mirror. A sheet of softboard divided this room from the cooking *coin* which consisted of two cupboards, a small gas stove such as is used in caravans and camping, a sink with cold water. Just inside the door of the room, through a wooden door, was the lavatory with rusted cistern and broken downpipe sealed with Sellotape and string, a small washbasin with two taps, one labelled COLD, out of which cold water flowed, the other HOT out of which nothing flowed. Beneath the basin, set on a frame, was a small bidet. The room was one of four 'companion' rooms, each opening on to a long balcony and screened from one another by pot plants, ferns and geraniums. The balcony overlooked the huge tiled roof of a garage from which it received, through ventilation holes in the tiled roof, waves of fumes of petrol and oil and these, combining with the trapped fumes from the slightly leaking gas stoves within the rooms, left a permanent sickening vapour upon the pretty geraniumed balconies.

To the right were the mountains, bare rock, white light, lemon trees, grey olives, even the young trees born with their ancientness, their snow-stone colour, and the thin drooping leaves like willow leaves in shape, all the olive trees with their colour stirring in the heart like an ancient grey mist; that was the mountain on the right; and the decayed villas with rust running out of their blank-eyed windows and fragments of twisted iron here and there in the grounds beneath the orange and the lemon trees and the palm trees as if some huge public work, once conceived, had been given up as hopeless; and the dogs, the hunting dogs which could devour a man, straining to get your flesh through the rusted iron gates.

The sound of the sea, on the left, was buried by the

roar of the trucks labouring up and through the narrow alleyway to Italy, their fumes rising and mingling with the salt spray when the tide was high.

My small room was squalid. On the second day the lavatory stank. My landlord muttering, '*C'est mal, c'est mal*,' twisted a piece of wire inside the cistern, stopping the leak but not the stink. It was in these conditions that Dorset and Elizabeth Foster, the brother-in-law and sister of Margaret Rose Hurndell, found me in my second week in Menton.

—We knew we'd find you, they cried together, with triumph.

—You are the Watercress-Armstrong Fellow. And we are related to Margaret Rose Hurndell – her sister and brother-in-law.

I wondered why they used the present tense.

They waited, as if for me to acknowledge their relationship, and I had a strong feeling that I ought to make a consolatory remark, as if Margaret Rose had just died and they were mourning.

—They say she was a great writer, I said.

—We've heard of *your* work, too. Dorset was reading something about it only last week.

I smiled my usual stupid smile.

—We've come to retire here from New Zealand. Dorset's French is perfect. We wondered –

They looked at each other, sharing a secret.

—We've bought a large house and a smaller one just beside it. We thought if you'd like to look at the small one, and live in it while you're here, you'd be most welcome. It's the least we can do for Margaret Rose.

They looked around my small squalid room.

—These are not really the conditions for a promising young writer like you to be living in.

I agreed. I'm an habitual agreer.

—No, they're not really.

—We'll call for you on Saturday then? To show you the house?

—Fine.

—Saturday then.

—Saturday.

We shook hands in the French custom and bid one another voluble, *au revoir, à bientôt, à samedi*.

The Dorset Fosters had been gone only half an hour when further callers announced themselves, forming single file on the tiny terrace.

—We thought we'd find you home, they said.

—We've brought you the key to the Memorial Room.

The Ceremony of the Key, I thought. Wasn't such a ceremony carried out in the Tower of London, in connection with the Crown Jewels?

Appropriately, it was Michael Watercress who stepped almost in a military fashion out of the line to hand me a Yale key with a tag inscribed, simply, Rose Hurndell. The yellow-tagged key to Rose Hurndell.

Remembering my duties as a host I offered them all a glass of *vin léger pour le table* but Connie refused for all. The handing over of the key was an emotional moment for her. She herself was a writer and with her husband Max had written books and articles for the newspapers, but somehow their writing life had been separated from their ambition, and lost, like the tail cut from the lizard. The death and the fame of Rose Hurndell, the former rendering her harmless, the latter providing unscreened warmth, had enabled them once again to unite to the body of their ambition, and to bask, their pulses ticking with excitement, in the reflected glory. They flourished in her fame. They flourished in their generous attempt to ensure her fame. The sun must not go out. There must be no more winter.

—No. We won't stay to drink with you, Connie said. —Some official has asked us to dinner. Do you know, I think he thinks that *Michael* is the new Fellow.

—He does, Mum. He does.

Michael smiled his delight. Connie and Max and Grace were also delighted, but Max, to bring a little reality into the conversation, said, —I wouldn't be surprised if Michael *were* the Fellow one day. He's a talented young writer.

—When we were in the East, Grace said, (they had been in the East, and many of their sentences began with 'When we were in the East') —people were talking of him as the young Hemingway.

My confidence so easily flounders. For a moment I was convinced that Michael Watercress and not I was the new Fellow, that I was an imposter, that I'd been given the Fellowship under false pretences. After all, my eyesight was failing. By some terrible *over*sight I may have misread everything in connection with the Fellowship, even my acceptance, and my journey; I may have come *blindly* to Menton.

My mood was momentary. It passed. Still, to be called the young Hemingway was a compliment. I looked at Michael Watercress with a writer's envy; certainly I would never be called the young Hemingway. I didn't even look like the young Hemingway. People might mistake me for a waiter or a school teacher or a floorwalker or a farmer; they would always know immediately that Michael Watercress was a *writer*.

—So we're rushing to go out to dinner. Find time, won't you, to sneak along to the Memorial Room, and just feel the atmosphere? Rose Hurndell didn't exactly work there but I thought you'd like to go *on your own*. Just *feel it all*.

4

The next day I took the advice of Connie Watercress and paid my first visit to the Rose Hurndell Memorial Room. I walked up a narrow street, beneath a railway bridge, and up another narrow street that had once been a Roman road, and on the left I saw the notice, Margaret Rose Hurndell Memorial Room. A copper plaque against the wall gave the date of birth and death of Rose Hurndell and the works – *Letter to Procne, The Lemon Festival, Requirements, Rehearsals* – which she had written while staying at the Villa Florita which I now saw was separated from the small room by a wall and a locked gate.

At no time, I knew, had Rose Hurndell inhabited the small room – a former larder or *lapinière* – set aside as a memorial for her.

The garden was overgrown with weeds, the stairs leading to the small garden thick with sodden leaves and fragments of papers thrown off the street. Putting the 'Rose Hurndell key' in the lock I pushed the weather-beaten sun-blistered wooden door which permitted itself to open halfway: it had 'dropped' like an old womb. I walked in. I opened the tiny windows. The room slowly became 'aired' like old stored linen. Small chut-chutting birds, with whistlings and secretive noises, began singing outside. A cool wind blew through the windows and out the door, a between-winter-and-spring wind. There was an air of desolation in the room and beyond it. The water-spotted plaques, giving once again details of Rose Hurndell's career, were scarcely legible. There was a desk, a bookshelf, a few straight-backed vicarage-type chairs and a layer of cold along the bare tiled floor.

I could hear the long grass swaying in the neglected garden, and the brittle rustling of the flax bushes that some former visitor had planted near the crumbling wall.

Here, I thought, if one were a spirit or dead, is a sanctuary. With a sudden rush of wind, dead leaves, twigs and a scrap of paper blew in the door. The air of desolation, of neglect, increased; the chill, of the wind and of the spirit, intensified and I knew the peace that is most known when walking in a cemetery, one is contained within it, withdrawn as the dead are from the world, and listening as if from a great distance to the movements and noises of the city and its people. It would have been more fitting, I thought, had Rose Hurndell been buried here and not in London. Here, in this room, they had another grave for her, to keep alive her death rather than her work. A unique memorial, to pay a writer to work within a tomb! I felt, however, that if the sheer physical discomfort (there was no access to running water or toilet, little light, and little warmth – what need have the dead of these? – and in the course of my day's work I would spend several hours in this one place) could be ignored (though unhappily it could not) I should find in the grave-like aspect of this room, in spite of the roar of the construction machinery in the many apartments being built nearby and the constant close passing of the trains, all of which became somehow insulated when one thought of oneself in a grave where one could not be reached, a sanctuary for working. (I found, unfortunately, later, when spring and summer came with warmth and light, that visitors also came: everyone who passed, seeing the door open, came curiously in to inspect the open tomb.)

I stayed a while sitting at the desk. I was overcome by a feeling of sadness that is conducive to some kind of writing but not to the kind of writing I was preparing.

I went out to explore the small garden where I found a green garden seat which I cleared, brushing away the small wine-coloured squashy berries, and I lay down, half in sun, half in shadow, looking up at the lemon tree in the neighbouring garden. I closed my eyes. The sun came out again, moving quickly, and was on my face, burning. I changed my position on the seat. The sun was hidden once again behind cloud, the chill started again, rustling the flax with a brittle snapping sound, and the secretive small birds once again set up their chittering and tutting. I fell asleep. I dreamed. The wine-coloured squashy berries which I had cleared from the seat and which came from a tree spreading above the seat, began to rain on me like ruby-stones, ruby-fruit, and filled my eyes with red juices and in my dream I remembered my arrival at Menton and the blessing of the colour green which I now found that I could not visualise, being able to remember only the shape encompassing the green which was now being distorted by the overflowing of the red. It was as if I were seeing the after-image of a blessing: not necessarily a curse, but rather the source of the green blessing. I found my confusion increasing. I told myself that I was dreaming the literary dream of a literary blind man, just as those who write or dream fiction have invented a 'literary' madness which abstracts from the dreary commonplaces of thinking and behaviour a poetic essence and sprinkles it where the shadow of 'the truth' falls upon the written or printed page. When in my dream I thought, perhaps this is the way Rose Hurndell died — had she not died of a brain haemorrhage, a sudden overflowing of life-blood into the brain which keeps its distance from blood.

Half-waking I heard the barking of a hundred guard dogs in the villas on the mountain-side, as if a pack of *chiens de chase* had broken loose, as I'd read that morning in the newspaper they had done, and set upon their master, an old man in a mountain village, and devoured him, and I heard them coming nearer and still I could see nothing but the second layer, if you will, of blessing of green life, which was fire, and I struggled, and the slats on the green garden seat felt like stakes pressed against my back; then suddenly, I think with the dropping of the real wind, the barking of the dogs ceased, my eyes cleared, and in my dream I found myself looking at a painting, a French comte and two hunting dogs – how still they seemed – captured and framed in the painting; they were the huge black dogs that walking beside a man have their heads on a level above his thighs and inspire fear and certain feelings of excitement associated with killing and loving; they walk like allies, equals. I am afraid of violence, in myself and in others. A sweat of relief broke out on my face when I saw the dogs were held within the painting; the stillness was not to be believed.

I woke. The desolate sighing of the wind had ceased. The sun had gone down. I thought I must have been asleep for hours. All the colours of the world had grown a shade more sombre and a penetrating chill had fallen from the mountain peaks.

Hastily I shut the windows and the doors of the Rose Hurndell Memorial Room and hurried back to my apartment. In the gas-smelling cooking *coin* I made myself a cup of coffee.

The next day when I saw Connie and Max Watercress for lunch at a café down by the beach Connie asked, —Have you seen it?

I thought for a moment she was talking of the new comet which everyone had been hoping to glimpse as it was supposed to droop its tail over the Côte d'Azur at six the previous evening.

—No, I couldn't see it, I said. —I think it's a hoax.

A defensive, determined light, which I was to grow used to, came into Connie's eyes.

—I don't think that's the way to talk of the Memorial Room.

I was apologetic.

—No, no, I was thinking of the comet. Yes, I've seen the room.

—Did you *feel* Rose Hurndell there?

A lustful thought came to me and I couldn't help smiling. Then I cleared my throat.

—Oh yes. The place reminds me of a grave.

Again the defensive light appeared in Connie's eyes.

—It's been neglected of course but they've promised alterations for this year. Water, toilet, electricity, and so on.

—I shan't be able to work there, I said. —I work long hours and it's not suited to long hours, without facilities.

—Still, when the improvements are made, Max said.

—Yes, when the improvements are made, Connie said.

—Yes, of course.

—It's important that you be there, feel the presence. You do like her work?

—Yes, yes, I do.

—I'm so glad. It's hard to believe, isn't it, that she actually lived and worked here, that she went to the Monaco Oceanographic Museum one day, she mentions it in a letter, I believe her sister is preparing her letters – oh and you must meet Haniel and Louise Markham, they'll tell you so much about her. Her favourite colour was red. That shows life, doesn't it? From the very first moment I read her books I knew: here is a genius. My brother knew her mother, you know.

—Did he?

—We come here every year, on the anniversary of her death, in October, to put a wreath of red flowers and leaves in the Memorial Room. There's a small ceremony. Later, when improvements are made, we'll have a glass case in the room, with two of her notebooks (one has no writing in it but it's the kind she always bought, from Woolworths) and a handkerchief, some early photos, a copy of a certificate won at primary school for the best long jump – Long Jump Champion, just imagine! I think it was twenty-two feet long...

—Twenty-one, dear, Max corrected.

—I don't remember exactly. But it tells something about her, don't you think?

I agreed.

—There's to be a reading of her works here, in October.

—I shall miss it, I said regretfully.

—We'll be here. And Michael and Grace are coming. Michael is going to cover it for his newspaper in England. He's doing so well with his writing. He's not written a book yet, but the discipline will come to him, in time. Every morning all four of us straight after breakfast sit down to do our stint. Don't we?

They had apartments side by side in a gracious old building.

—Yes. Grace has written ten poems too, you know, and published two books. When they get settled there'll be no stopping them.

—I suppose not, I said.

～

The next morning I called in to see the Watercresses on my way to the bank (there'd been some problem with the arrival of my scholarship money) and I found the working in action. I hesitated to interrupt. Connie and Max had rented for a month a large apartment with all facilities including hot water and a bath, a bedroom and a living room and kitchen. Grace and Michael, next door, had one large room and all facilities. This morning all were seated around the large oval table in the big sitting-room. Each had a large white sheet of paper, and in the centre of the table were two boxes of coloured crayons. All four were busily drawing.

I observed them. Max, in his late seventies, was of rather stout build, with rosy face and military moustache. When he walked his bearing was military, and his accent was English. I'd been told (to my anticipatory horror) that he'd had an operation on his eyes and wore glasses that were a kind of magnifying lens, so that when one looked at his eyes one saw huge brown dog-like orbs that in their magnification revealed the slightest wave of emotion. I had a sense of unreality thinking of him with his repaired eyes and I with my failing sight and sometimes getting myself into the frame of mind where he and I were brothers, or father and son, that anyway we shared an unusual condition and therefore should have special insight into each other. I saw in him only his love for and pride in his son. When he looked at Michael, if you observed closely, you could see the magnified brown eyes quivering with love; they would grow moist with their love and pride.

As far as Max was concerned Michael was the genius, the writer – well, the talented young man who could be (it was not yet the time in his life when one said 'could have been') a writer, or a painter ('he's always been good at drawing and painting') or a composer and musician ('he has perfect pitch, he nearly took a music degree, he has composed hundreds of songs and pieces of music'). Michael's talents were indeed impressive and every time I was with his parents I was made conscious of them.

I watched Connie, bent over her sheet of paper, drawing with a large blue crayon, absorbed in her work. Her face was permanently pale with the kind of makeup which suppresses colour in the cheeks. Her cheekbones were high and rather narrowed her small blue eyes. She too was stockily built and dressed usually in a tweed costume such as New Zealand women wear to the horse races at Addington and Avondale, and her evening wear to the receptions and dinners for the Watercress-Armstrong Fellow was usually a dress of dark shimmering material, and she carried a small spangled evening bag. Her hands, grasping the crayon, were plump and floury. When she spoke, French or English, she spoke slowly, almost mechanically, with a swaying motion of her body as if she had within her some instrument for winding her words, in sentence-containers, up from a great depth where they had fallen or been banished; sometimes one felt as if they were extracted with difficulty, as if she herself had gone away down into the rock to hack them out and shake them clean − a long slow process which made her listeners impatient: usually Max or Michael took over the telling of a long story when the words to fit it appeared to be growing scarce.

Grace, as one who had stolen the beloved son, knew her privileges; retelling Connie's stories was not one of them. Grace, in this family setting, was the tolerated outsider whose slightest false move would change her to the enemy; the seeds of enmity had been planted with her arrival as Michael's unofficial wife but the rain- and sun-making forces necessary for their growth had been imprisoned within the seasonless weatherless world of the parents' love for or indulgence of their son. While they occupied themselves with their ambitions for life through the death of Margaret Rose Hurndell, they were preparing for the life of their son (and thus, ultimately their own lives) to obscure and obliterate both the life and death of Margaret Rose Hurndell. They offered Grace no share of these ambitions, particularly as she was evidently disinclined to bring forth a little half-Michael who could be used if the whole-Michael plans came to nothing. In the midst of these politics of permanence I felt as unsafe and foreign and brief as a mayfly out of season; or like someone who growing up in the world and acquiring all the skills necessary for survival, particularly the skill of finding some relation to the passing of time, with the kindly aid of darkness and light and the rhythm of the body and the use of clocks, suddenly finds his biological clock is broken and he is unable to read the meaning of a clock- or watch-face, and, worst of all, it is dark because his eyes are blind.

As I said, I did not interrupt the morning work of the Watercresses. I left quietly, taking with me a feeling of being menaced – I think it was when Max said *au revoir* and his huge eyes like the saucer-eyes of the guard dogs in the old tales seemed to detach themselves from

55

his face and swim into the air, suspended there like huge tadpole-beginnings, frog-seeds. I said to myself I would need to keep a control over my so-called historical imagination!

5

For most of the first two weeks of my stay, beginning with the New Year, the weather was fine and gentle, the air clear blue and fresh, the mountains compositions of white light stark against the sky. People crowded the promenades each afternoon; the marinas were packed with visiting luxury yachts and smaller family boats from Belgium, Norway, Denmark; windows were opened; radios played louder; the huge construction works on the many *immeubles* caused the surrounding buildings to shudder with constant deafening activity of their machinery and the air to be filled with flakes of white dust as if from a construction-generated snowstorm.

Then suddenly one morning the Côte d'Azur woke

to find itself forced to accept a share of the bitter winter weather, the wild storms that raged over the country, in hurricanes, avalanches, floods. The chill wind wailed and whistled, the breakers crashed over the promenades, the new apartment buildings, set with disastrous folly in stark-naked earth from which the trees hundreds of years old had been *déraciné*, began their slow inevitable movement downhill, with great cracks appearing in their walls and foundations and their topmost storeys leaning at a dangerous angle.

On these days of bitter cold and down-driving rain I went once or twice to the Memorial Room and sat huddled in the dank grave-like cold watching the wall of water tumbling from the terrace of the Villa Florita over the doorway of the Room like a cascade of unceasing tears. Then I'd return to my tiny squalid apartment and crouch by the radiator in the corner. At night I'd put all my clothes on the big double bed and creep under the thin blankets provided with the apartment, resting my head on the long sausage bolster, and listening to my transistor radio, its small white earpiece thrust in my ear. I cursed that I was a bachelor. What a dreary life an author's life is, I thought. Then I'd sniff the current of gas that came my way from the toilet *coin* and then I'd switch off the radio and close my eyes, and then I'd remember my eyes, and wonder about them. Then I'd pray fiercely as people do as a last resort when they find themselves on a sinking boat or a crashing plane: God, please let me learn to know the darkness.

One morning, after such a night, instead of waking into the usual absence of pain, and ashamed of my prayer, I felt a burning pressure above my eyes as if my eyeballs were being forced back into my head, and the light, at first, pierced like splinters through my eyes. Gradually the objects in the room became clearer, but the pain persisting above and in my eyes; I made up my mind to consult the doctor whose address I had noted in case of emergency. Doctor Alberto Rumor, 10 Rue Henry Bennet, Menton. This was on the day when Dorset and Elizabeth Foster had arranged to take me to view their small villa with the prospect of my liking it well enough to rent it.

The day was stormy; the waves crashed over the promenade. I could hear the sound of the waves as I sat, my hands pressed over my eyes, to relieve the pain, waiting while Doctor Rumor, who had made a thorough examination of my eyes, reported his opinion which he hoped would be confirmed by the X-rays and blood tests he was arranging for me. He spoke English to such perfection that I became convinced that my own English was 'broken' and foreign. He was elderly, with rimless glasses, and a dust-coloured suit, with the coat flecked grey. His chin was full, above a mouth that one imagined was forever moving – either in speech gesture or in eating. Every now and again he made small noises of satisfaction, tasting noises, with his lips, like a chef getting the precise flavour of his cuisine. He wore a huge watch, like a navigating instrument, which he glanced at every now and again as if to orient himself on earth.

He smiled at me.

—Monsieur Gill, he said, —you may rest assured your eyesight is in perfect condition, as far as I am able to judge. I think the X-rays and the tests will confirm this.

—Yet I am in great pain, doctor, I said, adopting the formal English of the foreign student who learns from Cambridge University entrance papers of fifty years ago.

Dr Rumor leaned forward. I could discern a kind of excitement in his gesture.

—You display, he said, —the incipient signs of intentional invisibility.

—You mean I *want* to be blind?

—No, no. No, no. You are trying to make yourself invisible, on the childlike theory that if you can't see, then you can't be seen. Like a child who shuts his eyes and thinks no one can see him.

—I don't believe it, I said, indignantly. —I'm not neurotic, hysterical, or whatever you call it. I'm a matter-of-fact person, my feet on the earth.

—A *pied-à-terre* only? He smiled. —Monsieur Gill, this disease is *real*. One would scarcely call it a disease, though. It is what is known as a collaborative condition. Are you a cooperative young man?

—Cooperative?

—Yes. Do you fall in with the plans of others, arranging yours to suit them? Do you try to avoid inconveniencing others? I think the expression is 'putting others out', isn't it?

—Yes, I don't like putting people out. I'm a quiet man. I like to get on with my work. I'm rather shy, a student, more interested in my studies and my writing than in social occasions. I've written two historical novels and I'm hoping, here, to write a third novel, I suppose what will be called an imaginative work as opposed to one that is historical.

Dr Rumor tasted the air about his lips.

—Understood. I see. I've not met a case like yours before.

I grew alarmed.

—Am I a *case*?

—Not entirely. You know history, Monsieur Gill. You know the history of the annihilation of races, and of annihilation carried out, *il y avait une fois* by geological biological meteorological epidemiological means, and of, from time to time, the planned annihilation of man or men by man or men. And you know the story of recent times.

—But what has this to do with me?

—Ah, they all said that.

—What do you mean?

—No matter. There's another form of annihilation, obliteration, if you will, of a psychological nature, practised by human being upon human being. Usually the victim finds a point of resistance, his own line of defence as it were. In your case...

—My 'case'?

— In your instance – *par exemple* – you are cooperating with your assassins.

—Dr Rumor. This is absurd, I cried, pressing

my hand once again over my eye as the pain became unbearable.

Dr Rumor was unmoved.

—There were known cases of this in mediaeval – and later – witchcraft in which people actually became invisible; *en effet, ils ont fondu! Fondu*! And you must know, Monsieur Gill, of those races of the world today which are psychologically *invisible* – it is only a few steps to complete invisibility. Monsieur Gill, I know nothing of your life but what you have told me. I can do nothing for you. You are not ill, you are not going blind, you are a sane man, I believe. But through a combination of circumstances, through being in a certain place – which must be *here*, this city, at a certain time, and in the company of certain people, you are on the point of vanishing.

He spoke so seriously that I did not laugh at the absurdity of it, as I was inclined to do. Instead, I felt impatient and my impatience grew to anger when I thought I'd have to pay a good few francs from my precious Fellowship to a crazy doctor who had dabbled in the occult and had perhaps read Freud's notes on hysteria. He had told me, however, what I wanted to know, though I had some doubts, now, as to whether

I should believe him. My eyes were perfect. I myself concluded that the pain was associated perhaps with migraine. Or something. I decided to endure it while it lasted, and try to forget it when it was mercifully absent. I had my work to do. At last I had in some way relieved my mind of certain fears.

I returned to the apartment. The pain eased. I found myself thinking again and again of psychological annihilation, of the *mood* of annihilation, of obliteration, which may overcome a person or a country, like weather. I thought, if a person's psychological climate, which, I suppose, could be interpreted as his habitual method of dealing with his life, were of passive submission as mine in my short-sighted world had been, then a storm of unusual force, a combination of aggressive personalities, could wreck him, tear him to pieces like wolves descending from the mountains upon the timid sheep.

Well, I thought, all this is rather obvious, in theory. But does it happen in real life? Storms die, climates change, nothing is permanent.

I had been sitting at the oil-cloth covered table thinking this. I had been sitting with my chin propped up by my elbows. I'd drunk my coffee. I was waiting for the Fosters to arrive to take me to see their house. I remember now that suddenly I felt an almost convulsive fear pass between my shoulder blades. I held my breath. I traced my thoughts of the past few moments. Storms die, climates change, nothing is permanent. I had a horrifying vision of the Watercress family, and the Fosters, and the Lees, assembled in the Rose Hurndell Memorial Room, feeding on the death of Rose Hurndell, nourishing themselves with the power of permanence which death has and which they so much desire. It was like a pagan ceremony. As long as they were together in force around Rose Hurndell and her death, they constituted a power, a permanent storm, which could strike the so-called 'innocent bystander' who because of his circumstances must join the circle about the dead and because of his nature, the nothing-nature of a novelist who lives only through his characters, must be obliterated, erased. The idea was so fanciful, and the reaction from the fear so overwhelming that I burst into laughter, and just then the Fosters appeared at the glass door, tapping and smiling.

—You seem to be enjoying yourself, Harry, they said, when I'd let them in.

Elizabeth sniffed.

—What a dump.

—Let's get back home, Dorset said. —And we'll show you a place you can really live and work in!

They led me out to their estate wagon, of the new plastic type, tangerine in colour, and we drove away from the frontier towards the Centre-Ville and just beyond where, at the foot of a wide tree-lined avenue leading to a little mountain village, they turned right to a tiny oasis, suddenly full of palm trees, where, on the tree-covered hill, stood the big eighty-year-old villa where they lived, and which they had painted hand-somely, and on the flat, near the entrance gate, the small villa with the dark-green shutters which they hoped I would want to live in.

I had not seen such a mass of green since I arrived in Menton. I felt again the sense of being blessed. The palms, stirred by a light wind, were full of movement, with golden globes at their base. I said to myself that Dr Alberto Rumor must be a madman to conclude that I, Harry Gill, the Watercress-Armstrong Fellow, was the cooperating victim of psychological assassins. I burst out laughing again.

—Come up to the big house, Elizabeth said, —and we'll have a drink and you can tell us the joke. Dorset likes a good joke. He's always on the lookout for one.

Her use of the third person to speak of her husband who was present seemed to me, in my new awareness of the prospect of invisibility, a subtle way of erasing him. I wondered were they happy together.

Almost as if to answer my question, Dorset said, falling in step with me as we went up the path, —You know, we've never been happier than we've been here. Have we?

Elizabeth turned to look at us. She was small and pale, quite unlike her sister Margaret Rose – I believe she inherited her build from her mother's side. Her eyes screwed up in the light. They were powdery blue and her dress was blue. I was to find out that blue was her favourite colour and she invariably wore blue.

—No, she said. —We haven't.

Dorset smiled, a slight astonishment in his brown eyes; he had been confirmed, and resurrected.

We went inside to the big golden-walled house, and sat drinking wine and talking. Mostly of Margaret Rose, her work, her life, her fame and her death.

6

Later the Fosters showed me the Big House and the small house. The Big House was of Oregon pine (they were told it had been imported eighty years ago from the United States and built by a United States family, keen royalists, who made sure they were in residence for the arrival on the Côte d'Azur of British and European royalty). It was built with towers and many staircases, like a building from some northern fairy tale, and in the short time they had been living on the Côte d'Azur the Fosters had themselves painted it, repaired plumbing, knocked out walls, put in windows, planted beds of flowers, masses of geraniums, daffodil bulbs. The sitting-room was spacious with the downstairs circular corner, corresponding to the upstairs tower, used as a dining room whose wide windows looked directly on to the Mediterranean, while the windows on the left looked out at the Alpes Maritime.

Dorset Foster, I learned, was English, and had come out to New Zealand as a young exchange school teacher when he was twenty-four, and in an Auckland suburb he met and married Elizabeth, also a teacher, three years later, when she was twenty. Margaret Rose had gone to England the year before. After their marriage, Dorset had a permanent job in a primary school on the North Shore where they made their home and where Felicity was born. Felicity was now twenty-three, married, with a small son.

Two years ago, when Dorset was fifty, he had decided to retire on a sum of money, left by his father in England, and go with Elizabeth to live at Menton, where Rose had lived, and to supplement his income by teaching English privately to French students. Elizabeth's father had come to Menton with them – an arrangement which everyone said would not work for a seventy-year-old man, but, Dorset said, in the twelve months he had been there, until he died quite suddenly, he had become a real Frenchman, off to the football every Sunday, down to the park to play 'boules' (they had given him a handsome silver set that Christmas), into the cafés for his wine.

—All the same, Elizabeth said, —he missed New Zealand. I think it was a mistake.

For a while they argued over whether it had been a mistake: they could not decide.

—And now Elizabeth's bringing out a volume of Rose's letters, Dorset said. —And I'm teaching English three times a week to some poor woman who's lost her husband and has taken up English to make her forget her grief.

—And you really like living here? I said. —You don't miss New Zealand?

—Not a bit, they both said eagerly, quickly. —And now we'll show you the little house where we want you to live and work.

They took me outside, through a white gate, and down a short path to the little house.

—It's spotless, Elizabeth said.

(I remembered the real estate advertisements in the newspaper: 'Spotless. Immaculate. Kitchen a dream.')

—See. Spotless.

Everything was brand-new – new refrigerator and

stove in the kitchen, new hot water cylinder in the bathroom, new thermostatic electric heating, new paint and paper, floor stain, carpets, dishes, cooking utensils. And in the sitting-room, at the precise angle to catch the light from the windows overlooking Italy and mingle it with the light from the windows overlooking the palm-filled garden in front of the houses, there was a new huge desk with many drawers, such as a novelist dreams of, overhung by a bright desk lamp; and on the desk, a brand-new portable typewriter. I could scarcely believe the good fortune – I do not qualify the fortune with a personal pronoun because then I was not sure whose fortune it was: I only suspected it might be mine.

They showed me the bedroom downstairs, with a small bathroom and lavatory. There was a bathroom and lavatory upstairs as well and, outside, a completely private small terrace overlooking the sea and the mountains. Nothing obstructed the view. No tall apartment blocks such as were springing up everywhere in the city. A park of olive trees extended almost to the promenade at the water's edge; and, although here and there the sea was visible only through the trees, one can never accuse trees of obstructing the view.

When they had shown me through the house they

sat side by side on the new sofa in the living-room, while I sat in the new comfortable armchair. Nobody spoke. I sensed that it was almost a religious moment and they were to be the ones to perform the ceremony while I, as always, stood in the accusative case, the passive voice.

—Well?

Still I did not speak. Then I said, feeling the inadequacy of my remark, —It looks very comfortable.

This satisfied them.

—You like it then?

—Oh yes. I could work here. Get my novel written.

—We'll call for you tomorrow morning. Pack your bags.

I must have looked bewildered for they asked again, together, —You do like it?

—Yes, yes.

—Tomorrow morning, then, at eleven.

~

The next morning at eleven Dorset and Elizabeth Foster 'collected' me and took me to the small house to live and work. I bought a supply of typing paper and began my dreamed-of imaginative novel.

7

Menton is a city of innumerable retirement dreams quietly being wrecked by reality. The lizard ideal of sun and warmth, the human ideal of unlimited leisure, of unbroken views of ocean, sky, mountains, trees, make Menton a promised paradise for all when reaching their *troisième âge* they try to follow the tradition of stopping suddenly their pursuits of twenty, thirty, forty years. This arrest of habit often coincides with a permanent arrest of the heart or, less drastic, the retirement of some physical and mental faculties; also, a literal re-tire-ment: a fatigue on entering the promised paradise, on gazing at the view of ocean and mountain. The illusion of, the obeisance to, time, from birth to death in oneself and after the deaths of others (and before their birth), dispose human beings to live their lives in a prison of images. Attaining middle and old age, feeling that he has 'arrived' somewhere, as if he has taken a life-train from one place to another, a man feels entitled to enjoy the prospect of 'looking back', of 'surveying' his supposedly panoramic life, of resting on a 'summit' to enjoy breathing and eating and sleeping in peace and quiet now that he has 'passed his working life' and 'reached' a 'third age'.

The appalling deceit of a language trapped by images, which are the comfortable refuge from the stark fact of the limits of human conception, is that man should live and die within his sheltering images and clichés of time. So he journeys through time, and, retiring from his life-work and looking down from his supposed vantage point, he finds he has not moved or journeyed metaphorically; he has left nothing behind in former periods of his life; he arrives, by a real train or a real plane, certainly, with everything he has been and known and felt and thought and with all his past human associations; his luggage is so burdensome he can hardly bear to carry it; and no one can help him because no others can see it.

Living a life of myth, within a myth created by

language, in a contagion of myth, man and his 'reality' of being are *infected* (see how one employs the metaphor because one is not oneself outside the myth): the life of man on earth becomes a dream. How can one begin to *know* and to *say what one knows*, to say what one feels and sees and thinks, and, in the case of a novelist, what others feel, see and think? A musician has the notes of the major minor melodic harmonic chromatic scales to tell all; or the twelve tones of the invented scale using the recognised notes – within this limited vocabulary he is able to 'tell all' of man's birth, life and death. A painter, within the spectrum, may also make a sum of man's existence. A sculptor, too. A writer, however, born within a myth of language, surrounded by, '*hemmed in*' by metaphor is able only to be, to be born, to have his birth. What follows is an onslaught of language, an occupation of the tongue and palate which slowly confuses what, one only *imagines*, might have been the 'truth'. One cannot think of it in itself; images rise in the mind: arbitrary images prompted by how one slept the night before, what one had for breakfast, or read in the newspaper, or dreamed, or glimpsed in the street, or remembered from long ago; the image encircles the 'truth', *clothes* it (the night had been cold; it was good to be inside, and warm, covered with many bedclothes), makes personal what one had *hoped* existed, like a star, outside the human mind. But it is not so, it is within, the search is, as in music, a projection and return, a tension and resolution, and finally a coming home. Sexologists thus describe the sex act and the generative parts of the body. They draw graphs; they measure, record; they too are *trapped*.

Oh but I had not meant to write in this way. The problem is too much for me. I had meant to write of those – most of whom do not spend their lives trying to explore the maze of languages – whose lives do not quite succeed in bringing them the happiness they had thought themselves entitled to hope for.

Thus the retired people nearing the close of their journey are faced with unexpected treacheries, of language and the decay of a myth which they inhabited as if it were the reality of their bodies, and the intrusion of realities, abortive because they too necessarily change at birth to myths, to feed the process of knowing and thinking. There is a tale told here, in Menton, of the Englishman who retired here and who had spent a lifetime studying languages. On retirement he gave himself the task (making a solemn oath) of speaking only in nouns and verbs. One does not know what images occupied his mind, but in his speech and, one supposes, his writing, he kept his oath.

A curious word, *oath*.

Nor does one know whether he was happier for keeping his oath – nor does one know whether he supposed that happiness was a reward of the search for the 'truth' in words. His conversation, I was told, included only things visible. He spoke nouns, pronouns, and verbs. 'I take tea.' 'I took tea.' And prepositions:

> *I take tea with you.*
> *They use the boat on the Mediterranean.*
> *There was a fall of snow on the mountains.*

All references to emotion were excluded because they could not be described accurately. There was no reference to things of the spirit: no abstract words – 'truth' was excluded in the search for the truth – no descriptions apart from those of agreed measurement, e.g. the temperature of the air, the size of a room, the shape of an object (round, square and so on), hardness and softness, where they were without dispute, could be discussed. Also colours, and so on. Everything, that is, acknowledged to be in common sight. No thoughts. Not, 'I think I will have a cup of tea' but 'I will have a cup of tea.' 'I will write a letter.'

And the letter when it is written, say, to relatives in England, would (I'm told) go something like this:

Margaret,
Your letter arrived yesterday. You wrote of your journey to Bognor Regis, and that the weather there was fine with the temperature eighteen degrees Celsius. Here I look at the sea, I go walking on fine days, I work in the garden, where I have planted geraniums, chrysanthemums, spinach, a small olive tree a metre high, beans and daffodils which will be in bloom in early March.

For lunch I have pot-au-feu which contains vitamins, protein, and vegetables such as carrots, potatoes, leeks. I drink wine with my meal. Also I eat camembert cheese, blue vein cheese, goat's milk cheese and a cheese which contains walnuts both as a nut itself and in the flavour where the nut is not embedded.

I write all this because, suddenly confronted by the retirement of people and their hopes for their retirement, and then hearing – I forget where, or maybe I imagined it – the story of the retired professor whose chief study had been Shakespeare and whose preoccupation in retirement became the stripping of his mind of the corruptions of language, and thinking also of the trouble with my eyes and of Doctor Alberto Rumor, and finding myself suddenly with a beautiful room and desk and typewriter lent to me by the retired Fosters, I developed a combination of hauntings which resulted in the ideas for my novel. And I began to write it, spending long hours at the new desk, sometimes visiting the Memorial Room, to work there in the damp atmosphere of a tomb where the small birds, however, always came to sing to me, uttering their secrets which I could not understand, and from time to time meeting the Watercresses, all four, in their pursuit of Rose Hurndell. Michael tracked down a woman who had seen Rose admiring a magnolia tree, whereupon Max, in a morning of family 'stint' commanded the family to 'draw Rose Hurndell by the magnolia tree'. These family sessions were a life-blood life-paint or -prose to Max in his openly desperate attempt to keep his son by his side to neutralise, by making a chemical composition of mother, father, son, the potent effect of the mixture of the wife, Grace, with the son, Michael. Max sensed his attempt would result in failure once the four left Menton – he and Connie for New Zealand, and Michael and Grace for London – and you could see a despair in his eyes, and tears sometimes, when he realised the hopelessness of his dream.

Regularly, the Watercresses claimed me, for a journey, for a visit, for a meal, to enlist my cooperation in their annihilation of me and their replacement of me by their son. I realised this. I was no longer afraid. The Fosters were more to be feared, I sensed: their mutual assurance of their complete happiness was beginning to show signs of collapse and they were looking around for a strengthening or repairing instrument. Until the Rose Hurndell letters had been edited and published (an American publisher had made a contract with Elizabeth) they could not give the promised stability. Unfortunately I, in the little house, was in direct view, a captive. And so they descended upon me. Where could I, Harry Gill, hide?

I retreated into my novel, I became the retired professor, and if you want to find me, you must look there, and beneath the spectacles, the rather shabby clothing, the skin, grown more thin and soft, of a man of sixty-five, you will find Harry Gill, living his pure life, unadjectived, unadverbed, fully nouned and verbed, and numbered; and you will read of the consequences of his decision: '*Quick now, here, now, always –*'. In the next chapter.

8

In my first week in the small house I invited Dorset and Elizabeth Foster to dinner, asking them to come at half past five. They came. Dorset brought a bottle of *vin léger* and a tarnished bottle-opener with which he opened the bottle. He set it on the table. I had cooked pork chops with tomatoes, potatoes, carrots, mushrooms, apples and spices, simmering them in an aluminium saucepan on the front left-hand side electric plate to which was attached a thermostat in the form of a *bouton* that switched off the current when the temperature chosen by the cook was reached. I had bought a Bâtard loaf, and made croûtons buttered with garlic butter. There were three kinds of cheese – camembert, herb cheese, and blue-vein cheese – set on a wooden board on the table.

Before the meal, we sat down for a drink. We ate green olives. Dorset and Elizabeth talked of the day, of the news in the newspaper, *Nice-Matin*, and of the little house. They asked me was the heater working. I said yes the heater was working. The heater was a radiator with thirteen panels, filled with oil which heated when the heater was plugged in to the electricity. The switch could be adjusted on a scale from one to ten, with a wattage from seven hundred and fifty to one thousand, a medium warmth. It was grey, with small grey rubber wheels making it portable as far as its flex of two metres would stretch without pulling the plug from the power point set five centimetres from the passageway into the hall upon a narrow yellow-painted skirting board.

—Keep the heat switched on, Elizabeth said, as, noting that the temperature had risen, I bent to adjust the thermostatic control.

Elizabeth's voice was loud.

I straightened and stood up in a second.

—I will leave it switched on, I said. —At night I will turn it off.

—Leave it switched on at night too.

Dorset's voice was several decibels louder than

Elizabeth's, although I had no instrument to measure it.

I hunched my shoulders quickly.

—Yes, I will leave it switched on, I said. —All day and all night. The sun comes up in the day, and the sun goes down at night. Day and night are distinct.

Their eyes widened in a stare at me.

—You have a clock? they asked.

—Yes, I have a clock. And now, would you have more wine?

They drank more wine.

—It's dark in here, Elizabeth said suddenly, again in a loud voice.

I drew in my breath quickly.

—Is it?

—Switch on the light. You must have more light.

I switched on the light. The connection at the switch needed repair and so the light did not switch on for five to ten seconds while I kept switching five times and on the sixth time the light appeared in the two bulbs which were set in candle-shaped holders on a wooden frame painted dark brown, with cylindrical shades painted dark green – the same colour as the house shutters – outside and white inside which had the effect of increasing the light. There were three such sets of lights in the room, making a total of six globes: the first two upon the white wall between the windows which faced the palm trees and the cypress trees, the second two on the wall above the right end of the dark-brown sofa, the third two on the wall near the window which faced on the mountains of Italy and the frontier of France.

—There is more light now.

—Yes, there is more light now.

—You must always switch on the light as soon as the darkness comes.

Dorset's voice was very loud. He had drunk three glasses of wine. His face was pink, turning red. He had a moustache, greying. He was small, dressed in a grey suit. I knew that he had been a teacher mostly of children from eight years to twelve years. He sometimes used words which only children from eight years to twelve years use. He was familiar with children's games, too. That evening he described a game of marbles while Elizabeth and I listened. But that was later, after we had eaten.

We sat at the table. I served the meal. We ate it. Dorset smacked his lips. Elizabeth sighed when it was over. Then we sat on the sofa once again and continued to drink the large bottle of wine until it was empty and

I put it on the kitchen table and returned with another bottle which I had kept in the cupboard by the bathroom where I kept other items of food and drink as the cupboards in the kitchen did not hold everything.

When three hours had passed Dorset's voice was very loud, Elizabeth's too, and Elizabeth began to talk of Rose and of how she and Rose had both written poems while they were young and hers, Elizabeth's, were longer with more words and had more titles.

—She had a love affair with a garage mechanic. His mother took care of her son Eric, adopted him, so she had no legal claim.

Dorset began to talk about the French and the English and the French revolution.

Suddenly I said goodnight to them. They finished drinking their glass of wine, said goodnight to me, and went home. They were laughing as they went up the path to their house.

When they had gone I sat alone in the room and looked at the light bulbs and the heater and the desk with its six drawers and the red curtains over the windows and the orange marigolds, five, in a small earthenware vase, which Elizabeth had brought in from the garden and put on my table. As the curtains were not yet drawn

I could see the objects in the room reflected in the darkness of the windows. I could hear the palm trees rustling as a wind sprang up among them.

Then I went down the stairs to the bedroom and after washing and cleaning my teeth and going to the lavatory I went to bed. Once in bed I closed my eyes to stop seeing what was outside, but I could not stop seeing it. I slept.

9

Each day the patterns of light in the room were different. If the sun did not shine there were no light-patterns. When the sun shone, window-shapes patterned themselves on the rust-red rug of which there were two, of equal size, square, on the polished wooden floor. The light fell also on the table by the window, on the orange cotton tablecloth printed with white petalled flowers with green and red centres, each whole flower measuring nineteen centimetres in diameter. I looked at these patterns from time to time during the day to observe their changing positions and to note, when the sun had moved out of range of the room where I worked, the moment when the yellow light was withdrawn and there was no longer window-shaped yellow light lying on the carpet. Night came then. The sky was grey with crescents of darker grey. The mountains of Italy always reflected from their white rocks a white light, although in the daytime large dark shadows, unmoving, lay upon the slopes.

From time to time the trains passed, the brakes squealing as the train prepared to enter the region of the station; trains from Nice to Ventimiglia or Vintimille as it is known in France, from Strasbourg through Mulhouse, with the words *WELTEN SCHAFFT* written on some of the carriages, and at night the Rome Express. Through the night the trains pounded more heavily on the rails and by their pounding one knew that they were long trains filled with people asleep in the first class *Wagons-Lit*, which are comfortable, or in the second class *couchettes* which had six in a compartment, three on one side, three on the other, each narrow, though I do not know the exact measurement. As the trains passed sometimes when I was visiting the Memorial Room, and the train after a long night's journey had moved into morning on the Côte d'Azur and many passengers had already disembarked and others were sitting upright waiting for the end of the journey,

I could see into the couchette compartment where the rugs and the pillows were strewn on the narrow beds, and the length of leather strap used to steady the passenger when the train swayed on its fast journey was dangling unused, and the narrow aluminium ladders by which one climbed up to the *couchette* (if one had the top *couchette* one's body was very close to the ceiling of the coach) hung, also unused, on the hooks by the door and window. I could see that the train which began its journey away in the north with the *Wagons-Lits* and the *couchettes* made up with clean rugs and pillows and the litterbins empty and the toilets clean, had overnight been used and had come to the end of its use. The sunlight shone through one side window of the carriages and out the other, revealing the dust-beams travelling with the train and lighting up the emptiness of the compartments. The sun was always a morning sun, approaching a midday sun, and its beams were hot against the windows. You could see where some of the passengers, waking into morning, had pulled down the blinds to shield them from the light. In summer the trains would be hot and the windows would warm up quickly and the compartment seats would be burning.

At night the motion and sound of the train entered

my bedroom and my heart beat faster, hearing them, and waiting for them to pass with their sleeping passengers who did not know that I was listening to the trains and who had never heard my name and would not know if I met them on the station that I had listened to them travelling when they were fast asleep.

~

So I spent my days, writing in my new apartment and sometimes going to the Memorial Room where someone had left a typewriter with Elite type (my new typewriter provided by the Fosters was Elite type suitable for manuscripts). To get to the Memorial Room I now had to walk along the promenade past the old town with its pale blue and green and pink shutters, and its mass solid with not a sight of trees or streets between, the only growth visible being the row of cypress trees forming the boundary of the cemetery on the hill. Looking up I could see the rows of tombstones. I said to myself that one day I would walk to the cemetery and inspect the graves and the gravestones.

Each day I did almost the same thing. I woke. I opened the dark green shutters of my bedroom window.

I washed and dressed. I went to the restaurant, which was always crowded with workers having *petit déjeuner*, for the newspaper, *Nice-Matin*. I walked home and read the newspaper, choosing what to read from the headlines. I read the local news and advertisements of Nice, Monaco, Menton and the small mountain villages and the seaside places between these larger towns. I read the births and the names of the newly born and their parents. I read the deaths and took note of the ages of those who had died. I read the page of foreign news, the page of traffic accidents, robberies, holdups, murders, the weather with the temperature in France and Europe and beyond, the television programmes although I did not have a television, and the radio programmes, taking note of the classical and modern music and what time it was to be played, although I never listened to it. I read the answers to queries about the rights of tenant and landlord and the problems of those with widow's and old-age pensions. I read the list of blood-donors who had been awarded a medal or congratulations for releasing a certain amount of blood. Then in the classified advertisements I read the offers of employment for *Gens de Maison*; villas for sale; offers and demand for furnished accommodation; the legal notices; miscellaneous advertisements; animals; lost and found; and sometimes the marriage column. Then I'd read the back page which would have a late news story of a murder or robbery or the story, continued, of a disaster which had half-filled the front page.

After reading the newspaper I sat down to write, looking out of the window from time to time at the palm trees and the mountains. I wrote all morning after which I made myself lunch, pottered around the small house keeping it in order as I had promised to do, sweeping the carpet with the carpet sweeper and so on. Or if the weather were fine I washed my shirt and socks and pegged them on the clothes line that was strung over the private terrace; and being up there and in the sun I'd stretch out in the green deckchair, which had the name of a hotel in Venice on the back, and I'd close my eyes and sleep a while or lie looking down over the olive grove to the water.

Later in the day when people began to stir again after their meal, I'd go on the promenade and join the throngs of people walking up and down beside the sea. Then when four o'clock came I had the opportunity to call on the one or two English inhabitants of the city who had told me they 'took tea' at four o'clock and if I were walking that way I could join them. This was how I came to meet Haniel and Louise Markham, who had arrived from London about the same time as I arrived from New Zealand. Their apartment overlooked the Casino, and the avenue of oranges.

I knew the ages of Haniel and Louise because someone had told me; I think it was Connie Watercress. Haniel who had known Rose Hurndell in his early twenties when he married was now thirty-nine. Louise was forty-seven. He was tall, slim with golden hair thinning to an ash grey. His face was delicately constructed and pale. His mouth was small and red-lipped. He was clean shaven. He moved with grace and his voice was soft. Louise had put on weight. (I had seen a photograph of her in her younger days.) She was stout, dressed in a brown costume with a cream-coloured blouse and a tie. Although her arms were not long in proportion to her body, her reach was long as her shoulders were wide and powerfully built and acted as an effective hinge when she leaned forward to grasp her teacup or the plate of cakes that she had made, round volcano-shaped pastries with a preserved cherry swimming in its lake of red syrup on each peak.

Haniel and Louise introduced me to Harvey

Pulsifer, who had arrived that afternoon from America for a skiing holiday in one of the local resorts. He and Haniel, whom he had known in London when he was there as an economics student, were leaving the next day for one of the mountain villages. Haniel said he did not ski himself but he was accompanying his friend.

Before ten minutes of my visit had passed we began to speak of Rose Hurndell.

—My wife was her constant companion, Haniel said.

His eyes were small and pale blue. He concentrated them on his wife's face. His head leaned forward a little.

Louise laughed rather loudly.

—Rose and I were great chums, she said. —I looked after her. We came down here in the late fifties. Haniel said, 'Go with her to Menton, to the Villa Florita.' And I did.

—I was in London then, wasn't I, with my parents. It was my last year at school. I met Haniel at the Victoria and Albert, Harvey said.

—I was looking at the china. And I moved to the glass room.

—I was in the glass room.

Just then Louise clattered her teacup, and spilled

a little of the tea, about two spoonsful, on the blue carpet.

Harvey jumped to his feet and went to the small kitchen and returned with a cloth. He bent to the carpet and rubbed at it hard because it was an error. He erased it at last.

He stood up.

—Now, he said, —it does not show.

We each inspected it to see if it showed. We agreed it did not.

—So you are the new Watercress-Armstrong Fellow, Louise said, stretching out her wide foot and making a last rubbing movement upon the tea stain. —Are you going to write about Rose?

As she spoke I saw the muscles in her throat tighten.

—No, I hadn't planned to.

—Her sister Elizabeth is here. She and her husband have retired here. Elizabeth is editing her letters. You know?

—Yes, I said. —I'm living in their small house.

—Oh, you are! We had thought of asking you would you live here. There's a complete apartment downstairs. Private. Quite complete. You would not have to know we were above you. I don't have a very light tread but I take care. Haniel has a light tread. And we don't play musical instruments. A record now and again in the evening. If you are changing your apartment again, then, there's our apartment downstairs. Shall we show it to you?

I said that I would not be moving immediately from where I was.

—And you're writing a novel. We've read about you. You write historical novels. Are you a bestseller?

My book *Wairau Days* had been a bestseller in New Zealand.

—One of my books sold quite well, I said.

Just then Haniel finished his cup of tea and he and Harvey, with a smile and a pleased to have met you, left the room.

—These men! Louise sighed as she watched them go.

I had not seen such a used face since I looked on the old maid of all work at the hotel where I stayed.

—I'm a busy woman, Louise said. —I miss Rose of course. And Haniel's only a boy, really. He was on the stage in London.

—Really?

—Yes.

—Did Rose Hurndell have false teeth? I asked suddenly.

Louise replied calmly.

—She had the top ones out when she first came to London. He was a good dentist. But things have changed.

—Yes, things have changed. I'm English too. At least I was born there.

—Were you? What part?

—Sussex.

—Oh.

—I must go now, I said, standing.

—Your time is your own, Louise said. Her lips made a tasting motion and she made a sour face.

—It isn't, you know, I said. —You have spoken the first lie in approximately three thousand words. My time is my own! Should I be grateful to you for the lie?

She looked confused; she did not understand me.

—I have a big powerful car, she said. —I will drive you home.

—No, I said. —I will walk.

I walked back.

10

A week later I made my visit to George and Liz Lee,
in their home on the road to the mountain village
of Sainte-Agnès. They too had invited me for tea. I
caught the three o'clock bus from the Gare Routière
not far from the railway station and sat myself in a
back seat where I would not be disturbed by passengers
joining and leaving the bus en route. The weather had
been fine for seven days although a storm and lowered
temperatures were predicted for the next morning. I
could see the clouds massing over the mountains.

The road was narrow, with scarcely enough room
for oncoming traffic to pass, and the ravines were steep
with the road falling immediately from its edge into a
tangle of wild woods, mimosa trees, olive trees, and,

along the rising slopes, the grey cloud of the many lavender bushes, seen as a cloud in spite of the fact that I wore my glasses.

Without my glasses all shapes were blurred. This duality of seeing posed a problem for me if I were to carry out my plan of describing only what was external and visible, the common property of human sight. For instance, when I looked from my window in the early morning when I had just got up I could see clearly on the roof of a villa about a hundred metres away two human figures pointing and gesticulating and some-times leaning close, and in the imperceptible change from seeing to supposing I might have reported that I saw two people, up early, as I was, to enjoy the morning and look out over the sea from the best vantage point – the roof of their apartment. When I put on my glasses, however, I could see clearly that I had been looking at two tall narrow chimneys standing side by side. And if my sight worsened, as I feared it would, how could I be sure that the two people which had become two chim-neys would not become, with each deterioration of sight, completely different yet faithfully observed objects? Or if I found myself an optician who provided me with glasses of increasing power, even beyond the power of binoculars, even microscopic power, and I described what I saw 'with my own eyes', what then would the two chimneys become – a moving mass of molecules, a city with a population of stony particles, furiously in motion? And if I looked out of my window then and wrote:

> From my window I see a city of stone, with
> a population of stone particles, a restless city
> forever in motion, a perpendicular city which
> fills the sky and is on fire at its centre, a
> controlled fire which emerges from the heights
> in hyphen-shaped smoke ribboned in the colours
> of the spectrum. There is no light as we know
> it in the city. It is a rainbow city, a city of the
> analysis of light.

If I were to describe those two people and two chimneys thus, would you say I was being 'truthful'?

I thought of this problem as I travelled in the bus to Sainte-Agnès. My three thousand words without adjectives, without judgment, feeling, thinking, had almost been destroyed by Louise Markham's time-image from within the convention of the myth.

—Your time is your own.

I was shocked, too, by the revelation, only that morning, that the couple who regularly admired the early view from the rooftop over the sea were nothing but two chimneys standing side by side.

As the bus neared the side road halfway up the mountains where George and Liz Lee had instructed me to stop, I *made up my mind*, for my visit to them, to effect a mental change in the magnification of my vision – I'm not sure by how many centimetres, as if my eyes being binoculars I revolved their lenses to a point where, had I been again looking at the chimneys, I would not have seen them; instead, I would have seen the city of stone.

Of course as soon as I descended from the bus I was overcome by a wave of sickness as the earth rushed its brown and green mass in my face. Hastily I reduced my magnification by half. I could only just walk now. I walked straight into George Lee who had been waiting at the bus stop.

—Angela will be livid, he said.

I apologised and said I'd had an attack of motion sickness.

—Angela will be livid.

—Yes, my eyes do trouble me at times.

He was immense and ugly and his green flecked sports jacket lay in the corner of my eye like a public park which moved every time he moved his arm in walking.

—Angela will be livid.

He pointed to the small villa, something of the same construction as the Foster's small house but, presented to me, it waved in my face like a patchwork quilt. Again I modified my magnification and I was pleased to find it was just comfortable enough for me to be received as a visitor without my alarming my hosts by making too many defensive gestures and confused movements in the face of the oncoming material world, which was not now in focus, so that it moved perpetually, although it had a tendency to aggressive looming.

Liz Lee was waiting at the gate.

—Angela will be livid, George said to her.

—I'm glad it was on time, she said. —Come into the house.

I admired the view.

—How can houses be built here so high up the mountain? I asked.

—Angela will be livid, George explained.

—Yes, Liz continued. —By donkeys; everything was brought up that way, it was the only means of transport in those days.

Her face was freshly made up like a garden, red lips, red cheeks and blue around her eyes; it was new makeup, but I could see that of yesterday, the day before, the month before, the year before, going back I suppose to the seven years when the skin is reported to be changed, like linen.

Her gestures were eager, quick; her eyes bright; she was the middle-aged woman (she was fifty-six, I knew, and he was sixty-six), full of energy which fed her the illusion of being young. She had busy, narrow arms, and elbows that jerked about like angled branches in a fierce wind. She had been described to me as a 'dynamo'.

He was almost bald. His face was flushed, his eyes a little confused and his mouth seemingly without any power, which made his speech unintelligible, as I have described. Liz understood what he said and understood that his listeners were confused, therefore she was inclined to explain his longer speeches.

After a while, instead of the usual 'Angela will be livid', I was able to discern the words 'old' and 'retired'.

When the teacups had been set out (those

flower-bordered craters) on their saucers (truly *soucoupes volantes!*) and filled with clay and hot water which was stirred with a spoon (a silver garden implement), and I had admired the house and the view, and pointed to one or two books on the bookshelf (a cliff with ordered crevices neatly filled with brown gold and red bricks which opened and were leaved with rectangular white sheets, *deux place*, double sheets, starched and stained where some child or children had evidently played a curious game of catching flies and other small insects, breaking off their legs and antennae, and arranging them in rows upon the bedsheets, then pressing them, one sheet upon the other, so that they emerged in orderly rows, resembling a cipher), and we had begun to drink our tea, Liz and George, working together to get the highest degree of intelligibility, explained that they wondered if they had made a mistake in coming to live on a mountainside at their time of life. Physical ills were besetting them. The city was so far away; everything was beginning to seem out of reach. It depressed George. Liz made sure that she traced the source of depression to George. She felt more optimistic.

—Angela will be livid, George said. —Old, retired. Liz agreed.

—It's not easy to come out from England and retire here, giving up your pension, living in a foreign land.

—Angela will be livid.

—Yes, and on a mountain-side with so far to go for supplies and the winters getting colder and the shortage of petrol. And the ills of approaching age.

Clearly both felt they had made a mistake but they were powerless to change it, almost as if they had given birth to their mistake and now it had become a separate being which they could not touch or influence; all they could do was claim ownership of it.

One enjoyment, however, was the English library where George and Liz acted as voluntary librarians when the library was open three times a week in an anteroom of the English church.

—Angela will be livid. Old, retired.

—Yes, it's a great satisfaction, Liz interpreted.

Then she leaned towards me, like a doll-tower with her garden face and decaying olive-tree hair.

—What about you? You know I'm Head of the Welcoming Committee?

—Yes, you met me at the station.

—Did I? So I did. So I did. It seems so long ago. Are you settling down? Working?

—More or less.

—You will have seen that apartment, quite self-contained, that we have on the second floor? We never go up there. We don't care for the stairs. Living on a mountain-side is enough climbing for us. You would be welcome to live in it, Harry. Very welcome. Now that George can't always get into town, it would be company for him to have someone living upstairs. We'd love to have you. I think we met Rose Hurndell once when we were here years ago. A pretty little thing.

—I thought she was quite tall.

—She wasn't, was she, George? Wasn't Rose Hurndell thin and quite small?

—Angela will be livid, George said, helping himself to a triangular bandage of bread packed with sardines.

—I must be thinking of someone else. George says she *was* quite tall. One didn't know, then, that she would be so famous. She was living with Louise Markham, a bit of an Amazon, don't you think?

—*Her time is her own*, I said slyly.

—Time?

Liz suddenly became agitated.

—Both George and I have this feeling that time has cheated us.

Instantly she seemed to regret what she was saying, at least to regret her expression of her feeling.

She was about to say something further, then she sighed and said, vaguely, —You know.

In the words she uttered, *you know*, she put, because she could not bear to say it, a feeling of nothingness.

I did know.

To have lived so long with time and to find, when one thought one had *all the time in the world*, that time had deserted, disappeared.

I knew she did not mean to convey that time was short, that now they had retired they found themselves feeling their age and thinking of death and perhaps preparing for it and realising that their time on earth alive was almost finished. She meant that time had abandoned them, had been unfaithful in its myth which had given them faithful attendance as far as they could remember. There was *no* time now. Like a vanished occupant of a favourite chair, or room or seat in the sun, it left an emptiness which itself had become the intolerable if contradictory presence of nothingness. The lie had discovered them before they discovered the lie.

—You *do* know, don't you?

I told her, yes, I did know.

—And will you come to live in the apartment? You can catch the bus each day to the Memorial Room – I believe that a condition of the Fellowship is that you work in the room once or twice a week.

—Yes. But I have somewhere to stay, thank you. I've moved to the Foster's small villa.

They were angry, as I had sensed that the Watercresses, the Markhams, had been angry.

—Everyone is offering me a place to live, I said.

—The others too? The Watercresses, the Markhams?

—Yes.

Liz frowned.

—Angela will be livid, George said. Then he added, —Old, retired.

11

The library performed a similar function to the English church – it gathered together the exiles who had left England partly because they did not wish to be gathered together but who had changed their mind once they had arrived on the Côte d'Azur, settled in their retirement homes or apartments, redecorated and furnished the interior, cleaned up and planted the garden, and then sitting back to enjoy the arrival of the long-anticipated time for living, found that it was late, or it had been and gone, or it was only a dream. Instead, they saw the empty white winter sky, the bare hostile mountains, Italian and French, and another country's ocean, and olive trees, palm trees, orchards lit with oranges and lemons, all of which they had known as visitors before they chose their place of retirement, and which they'd looked forward to seeing daily and possessing. Gradually they became aware of the changed relationship, of the intrusions of intimacy which adoption, of a person or a place, forced upon the new parent, of responsibilities and shames such as members of a family feel, of frustrations and longings for release that are part of the feeling towards a native land. And this, with no rescue or assistance from the benevolent promised time.

It was at that stage the exiles began going to the church and the library and the British Association. They began 'taking tea' at four each day in one another's homes. They drew apart from the French community and became a tolerated eccentric 'little England'. No one should have been startled, on entering the English library between the hours of nine and eleven on Tuesday, Thursday, or Saturday morning, to find a collection of elderly men and women fumbling their way through book titles on dimly lit shelves (*The Egyptian Campaign*, *Italian Journey*, *The Great Generals* and so on), while talking to one another in Oxford accents, dropping names and sentences like, 'When I was at Magdalen', 'I knew him at Cambridge', 'The Vicar says...', nor alarmed to hear an elderly man or woman exclaim, 'Give me something light, a detective novel' (from the rows and rows of much-read paperback crime fiction), 'anything to pass the time. I just don't want to think.'

You'd have thought they would be thankful, as speaking of 'passing the time' showed that time was a reality, waiting for them; their problem, however, was to creep past in anonymity; they did not want, they could not bear to have the time for which they had made a contract with their leisure lives.

Among the small company you'd usually find George and Liz Lee, Liz energetically behind the desk, checking books in and out, George writing out receipts for subscriptions; Haniel and Louise Markham, though Haniel was seldom at home and spent much of his time in Paris; Dorset and Elizabeth Foster who, however, were not regarded as 'true' members of the English community who, when speaking of them, added in a superior tone, 'They're New Zealanders', which translated meant, 'They're not one of us'.

Also, during the time I write of, you'd find the Watercresses in the library – Connie, Max, Michael and Grace, usually searching for information about a topic which Max or Connie or Michael or (less often) Grace had decided was worth writing an article about, and they must all four get down to it. Michael's apprenticeship was being carefully encouraged. The Watercresses were not regarded as outsiders. They knew the members of the English community. They had visited the Côte d'Azur often. They had sent Michael to university at Aix-en-Provence to improve his French and soak up the French culture, and he had worked as a waiter at the Hotel Eugenia, in the tourist season. Also, they had founded the Watercress-Armstrong Fellowship. And finally, they knew how to pronounce 'Menton'. Elizabeth Foster, even as Rose Hurndell's sister, did not have the prestige of the Watercresses.

The person whose prestige most approached that of the Watercresses was the dead Rose Hurndell who could be talked about and quoted but not argued with. One knows that a tree sheds its leaves. In authorship, the author is not the tree scattering his books like leaves; the books are the tree; the author is shed, blown away, dies to make compost for other leaves and other trees. Rose Hurndell personally was decayed – the desolation of the Memorial Room was a memorial to her death. Her tree, her work, was beyond the reach of those who seek to prune or spray or retard blossom – but what shelter the tree was providing; and – who knows? – there might be golden fruit left, up there, away up near the sky, for the picking, solid gold fruit.

—There's always a chance, Connie had said, —we may find an unpublished manuscript.

Between the Watercresses, the Fosters and the Markhams, there was rivalry approaching enmity. I sensed this more acutely one day when I was visiting the Watercresses in their apartment and Connie mentioned that they had been enquiring from the woman who, with her husband, ran the apartment. Indeed, her husband, an architect, had planned and built them, Roman style (they had a Latin name) centring on a courtyard with statues, a tangled garden, and a fountain which gave forth no water into an artificial pool which was empty. Some of the apartments opened on the rooftops trellised with vines and flowers; everything twined and blossomed. Connie had asked to see a small vacant apartment on the top floor, opening on to a vine-covered rooftop.

—You must see it, she said. —It's just the place for you. The rent is not very high.

When Max came in from the kitchen where he'd been gloating over his newly bought *marrons glacés* and nut butter, Connie said, —Harry is thinking of taking that apartment on the top floor. You know, the one we looked at.

Then, when Michael and Grace came into the sitting-room, Max said, —Harry's going to be our neighbour.

I waited until the excitement had died a little. Then I said very firmly, —The Foster's place does me very well. I'm not inclined to move. Thanks all the same for enquiring about the place.

—You won't even look it over? I told the landlady about you. She's very interested in writers.

—No thanks, I said.

Both Connie and Max flushed as if I said something which embarrassed them. I had rejected their advances.

—That's the third offer of accommodation I've had, I said. —Not counting the Fosters. The Markhams, the Lees, and now, you.

—The Lees!

They appeared shocked.

At that moment, I think, their rivalry became enmity.

12

Have you sensed the nothingness of my nature, that I am as empty as the carriages of the trains that pass, dusty, used, in the morning sun? A novelist must be that way, I think, and not complain of it, otherwise how shall the characters accommodate themselves in his mind? To this you reply that it is he who must enter the minds of his characters? Certainly, but where shall he house them while he enters their minds, but in those empty used trains that pass and pass forever before his gaze? You see I have returned to the myth of the journey or rather to the myth that the frenzied molecular journey begins, goes somewhere, and ends, and vanishes; that metaphorical order must be imposed on the original invisible pattern of chaos. I must intrude language wherever I look and breathe, like the obsessive, trained resuscitator who seizes the inanimate to breathe life into it; or like the God who possessed this talent and, supposedly, used it.

I had been in Menton for two months. It was now March. The winter in its final convulsive display of life had arrested all transport to and from the mountains and through the country. Deep drifts of snow, gales, high seas, floods, once again became the chief actors in the drama outlined, criticised and photographed by the newspapers; once again tenants were forced to leave their *immobiliers*, threatened by yet another *déroulement*. Snow, it was said, had never fallen so low on the slopes of the mountains, so near the sea, nor had so many pleasure-boats been lost on the Mediterranean, nor had the Mediterranean been so treacherous in its impulsive apparently changeling storms of no visible origin.

Nor had the citrus crop been so abundant, and faithful in taste and colour. Behind special screens in the city's garden square, preparations were being made for the annual lemon festival, the artistic display of lemons, oranges and all other fruits of the region; everyone waited anxiously for the counterfeit winter to admit its nature; on the slopes and in the valleys of the mountain, the *arrière-pays*, the scent of the flowering mimosa hung in the air; the grey lavender buds began to open even from as low as the rock where they grew, to prepare the change in the colour of the sky that in three, four, five weeks would be challenged, rivalled, enhanced in its colour by the blossoming trees and flowers.

Everywhere, every year there is weather described as unusual, not by the visitors but by those who know best, the inhabitants. The old blind man, one hundred and fifteen years old, who lived away up in the mountain village of Sainte-Agnès and spent his day, if the weather were fine, on the stone seat in the sun outside his small house, watching the people, mostly tourists, come and go through the narrow cobbled streets, was reported as saying he had never known the snow so deep. He was not afraid to go out in it, he said; indeed, on the day he was interviewed by the newspaper, on his birthday, he was standing out in the snow, with an old straw hat pulled tightly over his blind eyes, wearing a bright blue nylon raincoat (buttoned), though he nevertheless kept raising his face to the light. The winter had been terrible, he said, authoritatively from his one hundred and fifteen years. And he knew. He might be blind – the bandits had come from the mountains, attacked him and blinded him, his family had descended upon him and carried off all his *belles choses* – but he knew how to assess the seasons from one year to another. His authority gave the city a sudden sense of pride in the unusual weather. The mayor, on a visit to Paris, remarked about it to a newspaper reporter and his remark appeared in both a morning and an evening Paris newspaper and was reflected back to the local *Nice-Matin*, like the effortless journey of a satellite swinging – as far as we on earth know – soundlessly through space.

Then, suddenly, for the opening of the lemon festival, the sun shone, the snow melted, and people flocked to the city – very old mountain-people, their mountain gait strangely unbalancing them on the wide, level promenade; guests from the many villas, pensions and hotels; visitors in fast cars from Italy and north and west of Monte Carlo, the rich-looking famous and the famous-looking rich, the unsuntanned and the suntanned; and the crooks, *les escrocs*, the pick-pockets, *malfaiteurs, cambrioleurs*.

On the days of the festival I left my work and wandered through the crowds. I was beginning to see a pattern in the systematic extinction of myself; I do know that patterns, in madmen or novelists, are enveloping shapes and powers; consequently I had a sense of oppression which was lightened by my meeting again Haniel and Louise Markham. Haniel, although younger than Louise, appeared so much older because of his frailty and apparent ill health. His face was very pale, his skin finely drawn, taut across his cheekbones. Louise was another woman of the 'eager' breed, with an accent not markedly English, and a conversation full of questions about the habits and lives of people living in the neighbourhood, which made her a gossip rather than an anthropologist. A rather rusted sensitivity served to bar her progression into tactlessness. I accepted the invitation to their nearby apartment for tea, and, as we moved up like kitchen parcels in the openwork iron lift, past the wide marble staircases, they asked me had I considered their offer of the small apartment downstairs.

Thanking them again I said that I was comfortable where I was now living but that if it should be necessary I would consider their offer.

The apartment, which I'd seen first on a bright day, now appeared heavily draped and dark with its maroon curtains and cushions and deep armchairs and dark-stained furniture. The bookshelves lining the walls were filled to overflowing; books lay everywhere on the coffee tables and corner tables: new books, with no price or name inside; some, I could tell, had been 'sent' without being asked for; others had been 'ordered' from England; others were presents from Louise to Haniel and Haniel to Louise.

—Haniel was at Oxford with Rose Hurndell's publisher, Louise said, as if to explain the link between the Markhams and their books.

—We are great readers ourselves, of course.

—Will you have China tea or Indian tea?

—Please, China.

—I always ask.

Haniel sat by me on the long sofa. When the tea was made, Louise sat opposite, the tray poised in her hand, unable to find a space among the books to set it down. I leaned forward, lifting clear Virginia Woolf's *Life* and D. H. Lawrence's letters and an old book, with the leaves drifting out, called *Mentone*. I glanced at one of the photos; it was of a scarcely inhabited coast with the sea directly washing at the base of the mountains, not, as it now was, driven back by reclaimed land that formed a promenade.

The sea would have had much forgiving to do, were

it human. The mountains also, deprived of the satisfying completeness of salty bathing and snowy crowning.

—That's a very old book, Louise said with some satisfaction.

We began drinking our tea.

—Now tell me, Louise said, a small juice of curiosity gathering about her lips – both she and Haniel, as some people do, like dogs, only more discreetly, seemed to be much of the time in a state of salivation. (It happens with advancing age, of course – what in adolescence is tears found on the pillow when waking, becomes a pool of saliva spilled from a long-used and tired mouth.)

—Tell me, what are you working on?

—Some work, I said dully.

—Have you got your *theme* yet? You do set it round a *theme*, don't you?

Living within the myth and surrendering to metaphor I could not quite decide whether getting one's theme was the equivalent of getting one's wisdom teeth, or a parcel in the mail, or perhaps a bill one couldn't pay – I worked on it, though, for several seconds before I replied,

—Well, it's –

—Oh, you haven't. I see.

She had not expected me to have my theme. There was nothing about me to persuade her that I was a writer.

Haniel sat silent. He kept making a twitching movement with his long pale nose; I could see the mark made by his glasses, though he was not wearing glasses then; the movement seemed designed to shake his glasses from his nose. The old age of the mouth and the eyes, I thought.

Louise turned the conversation, with some relief, to Rose Hurndell.

—We tried to buy the Villa Florita, you know. It is not for sale. You know I helped to look after Rose.

—Did she need looking after?

—She had a limp. She walked with a stick.

—She was not ill, though.

—Oh no. We never guessed.

—And you were down here alone looking after her? I said, as the novelists say, 'lightly' which really means with some heaviness of meaning.

She looked across at Haniel. He was indeed a silent man; he had scarcely spoken. Now he looked at Louise as if to say, you know best, then he said, —Yes, Louise came here with Rose. I stayed in Oxford.

—I told you that Haniel knew Rose Hurndell's publisher?

She knew she had told me. She appeared to be worried by her husband's silence and was trying to force him to speak.

—Tell Harry about him.

—There's not much to say. A very unpleasant man. Very pale face, bright eyes, dramatic manner. They say he changed some of her letters to make them more dramatic.

—Oh?

—She wasn't a letter-writer at all, you know. If it weren't for the interest in her – it accumulates with each article about her, each book about her books – but oh! her letters are full of grocery lists and prices and buying things; most unpoetic.

Louise Markham had succeeded in making her husband join the conversation. He twitched his nose violently and said, —Do you know, a letter of Rose Hurndell's was sold at Sotheby's recently – I forget how much, several thousand – it was a letter to a travel agent wanting to book for the ferry and train to Menton! That's all. Nothing else. It's madness.

—Of course it is, dear.

Haniel smiled a frail smile.

I thought, perhaps it was his time to sleep; that I had better leave.

Just as I was leaving, Louise made as if to keep me in the room.

—You must take some books, she said. —We insist.

I did not need persuasion.

They heaped books upon me (lent only), like many tasteful beautiful bonds, pulled tightly, and as I was standing by the liftwell waiting for the open-work lift to receive me, they asked, as if exploring another reserve of power, —Is your health good?

The fact that I was descending rather than rising, robbed my hearty Yes of its conviction.

I almost said, as I moved through the eerie dark mass between floors, —Very well, thank you, but I am going blind.

13

If I were to describe my state during the next month at Menton, I should say that I had 'settled'. I worked a little each day, I ate a modest lunch in one of the promenade cafés, looking out at the usually stormy sea, I took my afternoon promenade with the citizens and visitors, the middle-aged, the old and the sick in wheelchairs or leaning on walking-sticks and crutches; at times someone so thin, so pale, so moribund passed that I fancied it might be Death himself out for a stroll by the Mediterranean – keeping an eye on his prospects.

Then, after my walk, I'd return to tidy the villa, write letters, read, then spend the evening either alone or with the Fosters, the Lees, the Markhams, the

Watercresses old and young, going from one to another as each invited me: it was a settling-in period similar to the commencement of hibernation, I imagine. That month of March, following the wild storms, an oppressive stillness settled over the city and the mountains; there was not breeze enough to stir the sensitive palm leaves; no trees moved; the dead leaves that a month ago had rushed in whirlwinds on the footpaths and the yards, crackling like footsteps day and night, were shored up one upon the other in sleep. Day by day the *camions* with their *poids lourd* breathed the polluting fumes into the air. People in the streets and on the promenades looked tired, as if they had not been sleeping well in a world so still. The tiredness would be accentuated when from time to time a cold damp presence arrived from the mountains and winter furs once again were brought out and worn.

That month of March was vigil weather. The expressions on the faces of the people reminded me of the expressions imagined on the faces of those on land waiting for news of those at sea; people scanned the sky, the sea, the mountains, and the faces of others, to try to read the news or to find when it would at last be given. The Festival was over. The strangers had gone.

The town, although not empty, had an air of desolation. The thousands of fires of the oranges and lemons – so proudly lit and displayed in the garden square, as suns attended and grown in the earth, by those who might have imagined they had no need of sky-sun – were extinguished. On display for at least six weeks, battered by the storms, the fruit-fires that survived as fruit only were sold in an atmosphere so much in contrast to their late glory that one felt a sense of humiliation such as one feels outside the Casino at Monte Carlo, seeing the furtive notices in the upper-storey windows of some buildings – *Money advanced for Jewels*. There was a feeling that not only the fruit but the sky-sun itself had been robbed of its dignity, forced to sell itself out to keep up appearances. Does one become anthropomorphic over oranges and lemons? This time of oppressive still-ness, of tiredness, of waiting, was made more a time of cruelty by the dispersal for money of the once proudly constructed sun.

People were saying, too, that the oranges and lemons in the festival were always especially bitter, and it was not civic pride which kept the exhibits intact throughout the festival, it was a simple human dislike of bitter-tasting fruit.

The town was waiting. I did not realise that I too was taking part in the waiting until coming home to my villa, my sanctuary, one afternoon I found a workman's truck outside the front door, the front door wide open, and sounds of workmen hammering, tramping about, coming from inside.

Elizabeth Foster and Dorset Foster came to the door.

—Oh, Harry. We hope you don't mind. Is the place comfortable for you?

—Of course, I said. —I have everything.

They smiled with delight.

—We want you to have more. More of everything. We're putting in another heater. Just think of that. And hot water both upstairs and downstairs. And we're making a bath downstairs as well as upstairs. We'll install a new electric meter, to take the load. And you need a larger stove, instead of that cooking plate. We'd always wanted to make a few alterations but there seemed to be little purpose in doing them just for ourselves – we needed someone like you to get us going. You understand?

—Yes, I said, I understood.

—Now, you'll be here six months, Elizabeth said.

—In six months we can have everything fixed up, including a new roof. We need a new roof.

—It will take six months, then? I asked, trying to grasp the idea that the sanctuary for which I had already paid six months' rent in advance was to be disturbed.

—Oh yes, six months at least, for the alterations. Don't you think so, Dorset?

Dorset stared at me a moment, and I swear he had the look of a tailor who is trying to judge approximately your size before he begins to measure and cut – the cloth only, it is to be hoped, not the person who will wear the suit.

—Six months, yes, he said.

I felt, although he was sympathetic to me, he and Elizabeth were driven in this by a joint power against which I'd have no defence.

—What about my writing? I said boldly.

As I said at the beginning of my story I've never been a person who speaks up, and others have condemned me for it, for my easy-going nature, my tolerance amounting to weakness and described by others and myself in moods of exasperation as *spinelessness*, a description which man only and not an invertebrate looks on as an insult.

—Oh, we'll move you from room to room. We promise we won't disturb you. We'll be as quiet as mice and we'll tell the workmen that you're writing and want absolute *silence*, and there's plenty of room in the house for you to find a little corner of your own; that tiny desk we made for you will fit in anywhere, you'll be surprised.

I wanted to shout suddenly, —But I'm going blind!

Instead I asked Elizabeth if she'd ever thought of doing writing, like her sister Rose.

—Not anymore, she said. —I'm here – we're here – more or less to guard Rose's interests, not in a material way, in a memorial way, to straighten out rumours and so on. Our interest now is the two houses, to *create* something from them. I suppose if one were not being modest one would talk of it as making a work of art.

—Just as important in its way as Rose Hurndell's poems, I said, ingratiatingly, meaning at first to make an ironical remark but finding it came out without irony, almost with deference.

—You see, Dorset. Just what I told you, Elizabeth said. —Rose just happens to have written poems while I have chosen my own medium. Rose, for instance, could not have painted that sitting-room wall.

There was a pointlessness about the conversation which enticed me to continue it.

—You mean the white wall in the sitting-room?

—The white wall in the sitting-room.

I almost shouted suddenly, —But I'm going blind!

The workmen appeared at the door. They wanted instructions about where to put the new electric stove.

Excusing myself, I went out of the house and down the avenue to the beachfront and the promenade. It was too early for bathers but there were many people sitting on the seats watching the waves and the black-headed gulls riding again and again the large waves, and the *camions* tipping their loads of soil to make the reclamation for the new restaurant in time for the summer opening. The soil surged from the truck, some falling into the water, colouring the waves, the colour spreading along the waterfront so that the inner waves were clay-coloured, the outer waves the azure so proudly talked of and written of.

I sat on one of the seats. I felt homeless. The Fellowship tasted, not bitter, but sour in my mind. The springtime sky was blue, the distant mountains white with rock and sun. The waiting was over. I remembered a song we used to sing at school:

The glow of evening tints the bay
where cloudlets kiss the sea.
A tiny boat so far away
is sailing home to me,
is sailing home to me.

O haste thee home the sailor cries
I'm waiting on the shore,
Haste oh haste my heart it cries
the waiting days are o'er,
the waiting days are O'ER.

The final line was sung in three parts: by those
boys whose voice had changed, the girls and the boy
sopranos, while at the end of the song the teacher, a
woman, let out a long plaintive note, to the words *the
waiting days are o'er* while we echoed her note, after
which she (conducting the while) suddenly snapped her
hand across her face as if to break the spell, signalled to
the boy who was playing the piano (he would go far, they
said, and eventually he went as far as the corner where
he bought a garage, as he was an excellent mechanic)
who also stopped abruptly.

Then in a talking voice which sounded strange

unaccompanied, —Take out your silent reading books.

So I remember this. And why not, in the land of Proust: *Longtemps je me suis couché de bonne heure.*

~

And so, also, day after day, the alterations continued. Unable to work in the Memorial Room or the small villa, I spent my time roaming between the two, and hoping before I reached one, then the other, that I would find the retreat and silence I told myself I needed in order to think and write.

One day, a new stove, with a see-through oven, warming drawer, thermostatic control, light control and so on, was installed. Then I'd walk to the Memorial Room and sit in the tangled garden listening to the chuckling birds who knew about everything. Then I'd return to the villa to find workmen drilling holes in the wall to put in power points.

—Oh, we must have new power points. We haven't enough power, they cried, who were effectively controlling my every move.

Another day – new cutlery, new plates, a new set of

cups. A hot water cylinder, a new bath, a new reading lamp.

—You will want for nothing, they said.

I still had not told them of my prospective blindness; perhaps I did not myself believe it, for I had had a kind of obsession about blindness for many years, and even in my first two historical novels I took care to have at least one character (not fictional) who was blind; I tended, at times, to look on my preoccupation with blindness as an artistic device, like the blind man in a Greek play, or the old man or the fool in Shakespeare: the frenzied blind man who waves his stick and shouts, because he senses it, the danger that lies ahead. Even my parents – and my father a doctor, too – looked on my recent problems with my eyes as something that would 'pass'. No one in our family has been blind. They tend to deafness. Again, I was following a convention in not concerning myself with deafness, for even though a hearing aid may be visible, deafness has an infuriating secrecy about it, and it is harder to identify with the deaf; it is easier to make them the subject of humour, to make their comic mishearing of speech into a satire on human communication; and, as those who are disabled tend to do, they use the power which they find in their disability to surround themselves with an antidote to endearment. A hearing aid arouses less sympathy than a white walking-stick. In a way, by turning to blindness, or being directed towards it, I was following a similar path to those around me whom I was beginning to condemn both for their romantic notions of writers living and dead and for their uncontrollable desires to seek shelter and permanence in the dead and the work of the dead. Being in France, I was reminded of the scene from Victor Hugo's 'The Retreat from Moscow' where those who were victorious simply by their being alive could remain alive only if they sought shelter from the blizzard by creeping within the bloated hollows of the dead horses.

A fancy, certainly, to talk of Rose Hurndell as a horse, but I had seen her described as one, and written of as one, by a poet who had known her. 'And there was a horse in the King's stables: and the name of the horse was, GENIUS', was his prefaced quote from *The Arabian Nights*.

~

There came a time when the alterations were being

made everywhere except in the small solarium-corridor between the bathroom and the top of the stairs. I could close the door to the stairs, the door to the bathroom and the door to the kitchen and still have enough light from the glass skylight which was the only roof above me. I moved my desk there, fitting it against two of the three wall-cupboards, which I used as a linen cupboard and spare wardrobe. Oh no, I did not make this arrangement openly. If I had, my kind hosts would immediately have decided upon an alteration for the only space which they had neglected to plan for. There I worked secretly, moving my desk back and forth, and enjoying their triumphant expression each day when they saw how my desk and my papers were surrounded by the instruments of alteration. I say 'triumphant'. Had I talked to them of my interpretation of their expression they would have been alarmed and horrified, and exclaimed, —We're doing this all for *you*, to make *you* comfortable so you can *write*.

They'd smile and frown, —Oh Harry, you must think we're awful, but this is to make you comfortable.

Perhaps I was indulged as a child. I remember that on particularly cold cheerless days my mother would say to me, 'You don't want to go to school today, do you, Harry?' And I'd be tempted not to go, my mother's painting a picture of such miserable weather inducing me to shiver at the prospect of the wet and the cold and to think favourably of my mother's kindly qualities. It was only later when I was growing up that I realised it was my mother's need, her loneliness, which led her to try to keep me home on a wet cold day. She felt that by going to school I was abandoning her. I have observed this attitude towards people who write or paint or compose or in any way desert the living and the visible world to create a world of their own that is a threat to the existence and survival of the generally known world. I have known people to use all kinds of delaying tactics (and the writers, composers and painters and such like themselves use these for are not they as afraid of the threat of the destruction and recreation of the known world?), —Don't write today. Come and visit us. Let's talk. Let's drink. Let's make love. You don't really want to work today, do you? Don't desert us, don't threaten us, stay here with us, safe in the known world, looking at the sky and the sunlight, relaxing, after all *you're a long time dead*.

~

The old powerful clichés that don't even speak the truth, for death is the signal for immediate resurrection, since the souls of the living are designed as scavengers.

~

Therefore, while I condemned the strategy of the Fosters, to possess me, to alter me, to obliterate me, I understood their fears, for I had the same fears myself, but it has been my weakness or my strength or both that I am an observer, a nothingness which or who, suffering intended annihilation, is apt to exclaim, with interested attention, *I understand the motive*. My policy is disengagement; perhaps I should call it my impulse.

My fellow writers have called me a man of straw. I do not write political articles. I do not march in demonstrations. I do not make my voice heard against tyranny, injustice. In private life I turn the other cheek as I murmur *I understand the motive*, therefore I do not even have a claim to be a Christian, in the sense of a follower of Christ, for I make no protest to the boss when I realise that the work he has asked me to do will result in my death and when, at the last minute, I doubt the truth of the promises he made when he himself foretold my death. Being nothing, then, am I to join the ranks of the poverty-stricken bad poets who cry, 'I am the dawn, the wind, the sky', an assertion which has not even the properties of logic, since the cry is not also, 'I am a parking lot, a jet plane, a shark, a vulture'. Am I also seeking my own annihilation, as Dr Rumor believed? And therefore do I gather about myself a favourable climate and the people who will act as the prevailing weather? Then why have I not been destroyed before now?

These were the questions I asked myself as I sat at my desk in the tiny corridor and tried to write my fiction. I began to grow afraid of the new appliances. They were precious; they cost many thousands of francs; their instruction booklets, encased in plastic slip-covers, had the confidence of a well-advertised 'brilliant first novel' and the gloss of a record.

'Faites connaissance avec votre cuisinière jeunes foyers'
    Gaz, électrique, mixte,
    lamps d'éclairage du four
    cas speciaux

Allures de chauffe
puissance électrique
characteristic de brûleurs,
graissage de robinet de dessus
And for the refrigerator,
Prescriptions d'utilisation.

They demanded constant attention. Twice a month
the knob *de securie* of the hot water cylinder had to be
manoeuvred to keep the pipes from calcifying (tartari-
sation); a small *palpeur* on the electric stove which
acted as a thermostat had to be treated as gently as if it
were a human heart capable of human heartbeats; and
speaking of heartbeats, I felt them in the electric meter
when it ticked and tocked the hour – *J'ai dit 'tais-tu' à
son pouls*; now and again it was my duty to defrost the
refrigerator by pressing the automatic defrost button,
unplugging the evaporator, placing a tray beneath it and
collecting the ice-water; to clean stove and refrigerator;
sweep, scrub, clean; clean leaves from their whirlwind
life at the front door; obliterate, cause to vanish the dirt,
the dust, the dead leaves; take out the rubbish in small
plastic bags to be deposited at the corner of the street
by the railway line where the huge feeder-machine

swallowed them five times a week; sweep away crumbs, wash the smoke from curtains, take sheets and towels to the laundry, retrieve them in their plastic jackets, still and white; clean the bath, the toilet, with blue disinfectant and fuming bleach-powder, flush, clean, scour, wash down the steps of the patio, remove the dead leaves from the geraniums and support their few pink flowerheads against the earthenware pots ranged around the small stone balcony; geraniums everywhere; clean scour scrub; and bath myself twice a week, my allowance, lying in the deep bath and looking out the window at the tall tops of the waving trees.

Even then, when Elizabeth came into the sitting-room, as she would do, on some pretext or other, she'd stoop to dislodge from the carpet a crumb that had escaped the absorbing power of the carpet sweeper.

~

It was after my third month at Menton – April had just begun – when I woke one morning to realise that I was indeed *deaf*. It was no joke, no dream, no imagination; and so I would not laugh, wake or rejoice.

14

At first I lay quietly, trying to surprise myself into hearing a sound and listening with acute attention, turning my head this way and that to receive the sound waves from the air. There was no interior sound as of rushing of my blood or beating of my heart as I had supposed, in the rare moments when I thought of deafness, would be emphasised and amplified. I cleared my throat. I heard nothing. I laughed selfconsciously, Ha Ha Ha. Still I heard nothing. I tapped my hand on the wall beside my bed. I switched on my small transistor radio. None of these actions resulted in sound. There was a velvet soundlessness that was not even silence. One might have thought that it had snowed in the night, snowed right up over the brim of the world. An enormous fatigue came over me as I imagined that I would now spend the rest of my life straining to listen. I closed my eyes and sank into a nothingness which became sleep, and when I woke once again an hour had passed and the sun had set three narrow panels of light on the wall opposite my bed.

I was still deaf. I shook my head and began again turning this way and that to trap the waves of sound, but it was no use. I began to think of practical matters. Consulting a doctor, Dr Rumor. Then, I felt I wanted to keep my deafness secret. But supposing it was a symptom of a serious condition? I was young enough to feel that the only serious condition could be that leading to a swift death. Dr Rumor then. Oh Dr Rumor, I have this problem.

—Yes, what seems to be the trouble?

Then I realised that I'd not hear him, that he would have to write down his questions, unless I were able to lip-read. I jumped out of bed and stared in the mirror. I spoke, —How are you today, exaggerating the movement of my lips, but as I could not hear what I was saying, there was a distance about my image which frightened me. I heard, mentally, *How are you*, and I wondered if there might come a time when I could no longer have an image of sound, when the words *How are you* would become objects to look at as I was now looking at myself, at my moving lips, at the panels of sunlight. Then a more practical thought came to me. I wanted this Fellowship in Menton. I wanted to keep it. If some drastic physical condition overcame me I should have to relinquish the Fellowship and return to New Zealand. I decided that I must keep the deafness secret. It could only be temporary. I'd consult Dr Rumor. I'd write down what I wanted to say to him. (Deafness was already giving me a reluctance to talk.)

Then a sentence came to mind: 'The blind man, in his fury, struck out with his white stick.'

How would I strike out in my fury? With my hearing aid, and have the world laughing at me? How would I know, when I spoke, if my voice were too loud or too soft? I'd often been startled by the shouting of those who were deaf. (He's deaf, that's why he shouts.)

Beethoven...

How comforting to ally oneself with the great. *He* could still hear, mentally: auditory images were different, depending largely on memory, and as I was only thirty-three and my memory was good and I'd had thirty-three years of hearing…

~

Fifteen minutes later I was preparing breakfast for myself, standing in the small kitchen in front of the refrigerator and the grand stove with its glass-doored oven and its thermostatic *palpeur*. Normally, the refrigerator made a sound like a distant jet plane with a background of a high-pitched whine, while the stove, in use, sang a more subdued note, a low-pitched hum if the left-hand plate were set at its highest, ten.

The kitchen was silent. I was silent. My footsteps made no sound, the external world sent no sound through the windows; a loosened window-catch set one window swinging to and fro, and the slight breeze swaying the palm trees did not cause the usual shuffling of leaves as if unseen footsteps were following a path in the air. Presently I grew used to the soundlessness. A train passed. I felt the vibrations through my body. I felt the house brace itself against the assault of the train-sound but I heard no sound: my body received the news of the train; my feet, my belly, knew it was passing.

I wanted to get out, to get out of myself, to hear. I looked out of the kitchen window as I ate my breakfast. I was an early riser. Few people were up. The Fosters' curtains were still drawn. In the one huge apartment block beside the Fosters' one or two lights were on. Someone was rolling up a blind on the third floor balcony.

A middle-aged man. I'd seen him before, doing his housekeeping, carefully moving the table and chairs as he swept around them, and then sitting by himself to dine, looking out over the olive grove at the sea. Perhaps at this hour he was looking for Corsica which was said to be visible before sunrise, in winter only, though few people had seen it, and seeing it with little effort from two healthy eyes or from two healthy eyes behind carefully trained binoculars, gave one, in Menton, a lifelong cause for pride. Seeing Corsica was a 'gift' and as with gifts it was not a case of one's choosing to see but of being chosen.

The man in the apartment vigorously shook a mat over the balcony; I could see the dust flying, even from my window. Evidently he was not hoping or trying to see Corsica.

I know now that in affliction one does not think

grand thoughts: one's thoughts are mean, resentful. Not being able to grasp the fact of my deafness, I turned again to the idea of blindness, thinking, as if it might have been a haven, *Now if I had been blind I would be able to say, rousing pity, —I shall never see Corsica.* Who will have sympathy for me if I say I can never hear Corsica? I despised myself. I had become a living anticlimax. One does not always quote fiction as a good example for life but, I told myself, I would never have let this happen in fiction – a man going blind who instead becomes deaf, who, concentrating on the drama of looking his last on colour and light and form, suddenly finds himself robbed forever of the first few bars of the Hammerklavier Sonata, of their entering again from the outside world as if they lived there, in comfort and prosperity, as citizens of a respected country.

I had located my drama: Beethoven would take me by the hand through the paradise and hell of soundlessness, but first, because I was only Harry Gill, I would go to Dr Rumor and say, —Dr Rumor, I'm deaf, stone deaf, I can't even hear if the new refrigerator is working.

Therefore, as early as possible, and avoiding any meeting with Dorset and Elizabeth and beginning an acquaintance with the experience of being a Removed

Man (my mind played with the use of the word 'remove' in the serving of meals, and the controversy about whether the 'remove' should be eaten first or last; I had a feeling of horror as I remembered what I had read only a week ago in a cookery book, 'Hunger and thirst are unlovely things yet they are the foundation for the house of hospitality'), I set out to visit Dr Alberto Rumor in Rue Henry Bennet.

My walk was unsteady; I had not realised how much the sound of my feet firmly striking the earth had directed my ability to walk. I kept turning my head this way and that, trying to receive and interpret sound, working it like a radar tower, and my confusion increased as I felt my powers of interpretation working overtime on sounds which were nothing but imaginings.

I saw a heavy truck. I thought I heard it. I became afraid. I began to think I would not get as far as Rue Henry Bennet. I felt very lonely. No one knew I was deaf; I had no signal to put out for attention, sympathy and consideration. My hands cupped behind my ears would invite laughter or smiles. My incomprehension when spoken to would label me, perhaps, as one of the unfortunately disabled who must be arranged for or removed. I hadn't realised before how much of one's day is spent in talking to oneself, in listening to body sounds and movements, in uttering now and again small sighs of pleasure or pain, in exclaiming and hearing the exclamation with satisfaction, oneself talking to oneself.

It occurred to me that my removal was as complete, or seemed so, as if I were invisible; my feeble eyes, perhaps in a kind of jealousy or rivalry, emotions which I'm told eyes are capable of feeling, searched up and down, everywhere they could look, not only for the reassurance of my visibility but for a chance sight of some small sound to carry, with an emphasis of magnanimity, to the threshold, the pavilion, the inner chambers of my ears.

I was pleased that Dr Rumor remembered me. Even Hamlet's father's ghost, for all his demands in the name of memory, would have been pleased by the simple recognition of a smile. Dr Rumor was about to say something to me – he had begun – when I gave him the sheet of paper I had been preparing as I sat in his waiting-room. It said: —I'm totally deaf. Since early this morning I haven't been able to hear a sound, not even myself breathing.

Dr Rumor looked at me as at an object. He frowned. I held out my hand for the sheet of writing-paper. I took it and leaning it on the edge of his deck I wrote, —It's true. I'm deaf. Write to me.

Reading what I had written I had an impulse to laugh. Write to me, indeed. It sounded as final as 'Remember me', a paper utterance made before I set out on a long journey to a land where I would be almost inaccessible.

Obediently, Dr Rumor wrote, —You're the young man who consulted me before. The young man in the newspaper photograph, standing beside the Watercress-Armstrong Fellow.

I read what he had written. I felt erased.

He drew down the brilliant ceiling light and taking his instruments he began to examine my ears. He took out his watch and held it by each ear. He said something which of course I could not hear. Then he opened his mouth and made a grimace; he looked as if he were shouting for his jaw tensed and thrust out like a container for the sound he was obviously making.

When he had made all the examination he seemed to require, he raised the light to its normal position, took the sheet of paper and wrote, as if he were sending a telegram, —Can't help you. Modern disease. Auditory Retaliation. Strategy of War.

In answer to this peculiar telegram I wrote, —Self-inflicting?

He wrote in reply, —A sealing-off, a closure. Auditory hibernation.

—Permanent? A physical condition?

The telegraphic phrases were appropriate, I thought, for my state of removal.

He smiled and shook his head. Evidently he did not know.

He wrote, —Seems to be.

This was the moment, I thought, when patient and doctor would begin talking about the best specialists in the country, 'ear-nose-and-throat'. I knew. My father was a doctor. I had been a medical student. I had an aunt with Ménière's disease, and, while I was studying, several patients with ear disease or malfunction or, now that we are in an age of empirical drugs, malformation. I had seen a child born with tiny ears where its arms should have been, wheat-ears new on a green wheatstalk. The child could breathe and move but not hear or talk. The child did not live.

There was no space left on the paper which Dr Rumor and I had used, otherwise I would have written, I thought, —What shall I do?

Anticipating my question he drew another sheet of paper from his desk drawer, licked the tip of his ball-point pen (an unhygienic habit I felt for a doctor) and wrote for a few seconds, every now and again glancing at me as if, estimating my character and capabilities, he were writing me a reference for a job.

He passed the paper over to me. I read, —As I said before, Mr Gill, you are at the point of bisection of circumstances, opportunity, characters, time; every-thing is favourable for your obliteration. You have been stifled, muffled, silenced. You cannot cry out because you cannot hear the cries of others.

On an isolated line he had written: Interesting. As if it were in place of: To be recommended. Or: A good worker. Or: Conscientious.

I wrote, —But what can I do?

—Mr Harry Gill – is that really your name, by the way? Just wait and see. I think your condition will cure itself. I give it four months.

—Four months! And wait and see! What about, Wait and Hear! Hear nothing! Four months is the time of my Fellowship. What are you hinting?

—Trust me. Wait and see.

As I was leaving I put out my hand for my pen

which Dr Rumor had pocketed; his own was still in his hand. He apologised. I went as quickly as I could from his consulting room. He was as unbelievable a doctor as ever I had met. I glanced at the brass plate at the door to make certain that it had not been I who had created him and his unbelievability – no, I read: 'Dr Alberto Rumor, Specialist in General Medicine'.

How hard it is to be oneself! What is oneself? Always one must do as others are doing, even if it is the others who lived in a stone age or other ages than ours – even the old man finds his hero; the poet of seventy, who has written quietly, mostly unadmired, for many years, begins to draw the inspiration of his daily life from the letters of the young Keats. He reads Milton. He learns Latin and begins to read Latin verse. He attempts Greek. Suddenly, at seventy, he is satisfied only with reading Homer, Sophocles, in the 'original', this poet whose strength in writing has been his technical skill, his powers of observation, and not his originality. In the young Keats he has found, nevertheless, a companion and hero. In a year's time, if he is alive, he will have found another hero and model, as if he were adolescent again, and he will be saying, I'm reading X in the original. Y did, you know. I've been reading Y's life.

Only, because Y is dead, he is unlikely to dress like Y, though if he finds a physical resemblance to him he may cultivate a beard or a special way of doing his hair, if he has hair, which reminds those who know Y or have seen photographs or daguerreotypes or artists' likenesses of Y, to comment on the resemblance.

I myself had once relied on Keats to instruct me how to pass my time! I drank the wine that Keats drank. I did not care for the French language because Keats thought it uglier than the conversation overheard around Babel. Yet I have never been a person of extreme suggestibility, only, as Keats described himself, one of extreme nothingness which, given the talent and the imagination, would have made me an actor. I don't imagine that Keats and I are alone in this nothing-ness – it is the commonest state in its simplest form where it remains nothingness, emptiness, a container with now and again a few contents – Mr Metonymy, the container for the contents, where Mr Metonymy has no contents. The streets of the world are peopled with the Metonymy Family, the containers with few contents, living in figurative bliss, while others, desiring to change, embrace the simple genre, whatever that means, become members of the Literal Family, which survives through its centuries-long feud with the Metaphors and the Similes.

Here I was, then, newly deafened Mr Anticlimax, feeling like one of the species of writers whom I despised – those, growing in number, who must 'experience' their subjects, who will dye themselves different colours so as to 'feel' the experience of being of different race, who will work for a year in an office, live in prison, in a cave, on a desert island, in a monastery, in order to write their 'intimate story' of life in these places: *Third Trimester Bleeding, The Mechanics and Expectations of a Central Tumour, The Blood–Brain Barrier, Fabric Food, Catecholamines, Small Sample Problems, Multi-media Learning.*

I decided to live with my deafness for the period of my Fellowship, to be a deaf Watercress-Armstrong Fellow, with what must have appeared to be alarming disregard for my future health and the prospects of a cure which would diminish, I supposed, unless I sought help at once from a specialist. I could not explain, then or now, my *laissez-faire* state of mind about something on which my survival might have depended. When Dr Rumor suggested I go at once to a specialist to have tests taken, X-rays and so on, and that agonising test which is remarkably like water torture where water is poured into one's ears until one is on the verge of fainting, I wrote on the new sheet of paper provided that I knew someone and would take care of the matter myself. These were lies. I knew no specialist in Menton. I suppose that, thirty-three years old, not long technically out of adolescence, which for me anyway was a delayed process, I was courting disaster as surely but not so evidently as the young man who buys a motorbike and rides it at its full capacity. Yet I had never been a reckless person. Rather, I had been rather timid, bookish, cautious in my actions. It often happens, however, that with a person of my nature, the power of the crowd may suddenly pierce his perfect behaviour, and his nature is artificially inseminated with the potency of the master brute 'crowd psychology' or 'adolescent psychology'.

Whatever the explanation I accepted my deafness with a passivity which, before the age of the raging clitoris, would have been looked on as feminine!

Although I accepted this total deafness I was not overjoyed by it. I was depressed and afraid. Once again I knew the strangeness and numbness of walking soundlessly through soundless streets and of watching the mouths of people open and shut, pout, twist, beg, as if they were fledgling birds each looking on the other for food, which they were doing; I could see them receiving and swallowing words, rejecting them at times, tasting them, relishing them, then perhaps spitting them out as if they had found the bitter stones within the sweet fruit. I became aware even as I walked home to my *petite maison* that I now looked hungrily on the mouths of others, and I was aware of a survival instinct in myself by which my intensity of staring awakened gradually the ability to 'read' the lips so that even without sound I too could taste the words. I felt afraid that I would forget the sound of words. I wanted to anchor my memory as if it were an intractable giant and I a tiny Gulliver; walk the miles and miles around its vastness, winding, securing an unbreakable bond.

As I turned the key in the front door of the little house, and walked in flannel-footed from the flannel world I realised that I had half-hoped that in my home, at least, there would be sound again, that it would be switched on, the way electricity is cut off while the company makes urgent repairs and one goes out for a walk planning to return when everything is working again, the lights lighting, the refrigerator refrigerating, the heater heating; and so on returning, one touches the switch inside the front door and the light shines instantly. Ah. Back to normal. The feeling of suspension in a hostile dark machineless world, the obsessive wondering how it used to be when writers wrote with quills and went to bed at sunset, the loneliness of estrangement from progress convincingly equated with necessity, all vanish at the touch of the switch; one can breathe again.

I don't think I have ever been as near to crying as that morning when I shut the front door behind me and stood, hearing no sound at all, though I even waited for a minute or two in case last-minute 'adjustments' were being made to the hearing mechanism which I now appeared to think of as something beyond myself, in some central workshop where these matters were dealt with. No sound. I took a deep breath, which I had to take on trust because I could not hear it – I was reminded that in future this would be the nature of my speaking, if I tried to speak, speech on trust.

I went to my bedroom and made my bed. I felt very tired and lonely. I wanted desperately to think myself back to the day before, as if what had been visited upon me were a kind of punishment and if only I could return to 'yesterday' I would promise to be and do all that was asked of me. Asked by whom?

I would have to be careful. I was peopling the world with agents. I was fast throwing out my normal mental furniture and all the harmless inhabitants of my mind, and I realised that I was in danger of opening the door to find them transformed, the gentle inhabitants into devourers, the furniture into an expanding space-engulfing suffocation. (I was remembering a recent newspaper story of the farmer who turned his dogs out for the night and when he opened the door in the morning to feed them they killed and devoured him.)

I smoothed the coverlet on my bed, put out my pyjamas for the night. I glanced at my watch. It said half past eleven. I went upstairs to the corridor and sat at my desk, opened my typewriter and put in a sheet of paper. I withdrew the paper, closed the typewriter and, leaving my desk, went into the living room where I sat on the sofa and looked out at the palm trees. The day was going to be fine. There was no wind. The palm leaves hung without moving. I looked up at the Fosters' house and could see no sign of their being home. Perhaps they were gardening up the back of their land? They sometimes gardened in a fury for two or three days at a time, wrestling with weeds and stones and many years of neglect, and after their three days' work they would say to me, 'We're not really gardeners, not in the usual sense.' It had not worried me that, like many people, they were living in an illusion about their own natures – I was reminded of someone I knew who while insisting, 'I'm not really a traveller, you know,' spent her time flying from country to country. I accepted, however, Elizabeth Foster's explanation (their gardening had not only to be denied but explained) that Rose had been fond of gardening, and I was aware that when someone in a family dies, those who remain often adopt characteristics and habits of the dead as if these had thereby been abandoned, as orphans, which no one else would take in and care for.

—Yes, she did love, even as a child, her little bed of flowers.

And when I had said, for something to say, —Did she like roses? Elizabeth had said, —Definitely not, well, not particularly. Because of her name. She didn't like her name. We were named after princesses.

I said, again for something to say, that I thought that was quite romantic.

For something to say.

I was remembering it. *Just for something to say.* In a

dark dark world when it's too late anyway we think of all the times we have left the light burning and burning, not to see by or read by or be comforted by, just because it was a light which, at a turn of a switch, burned.

Then I saw Elizabeth Foster at the window. She saw me and waved. I waved back. I hoped that she wouldn't look on it as an invitation.

About five minutes later I felt vibrations coming from the back door. I thought, well, it's not earthquake weather and I'm not in earthquake country, the little house is feeling its age; it seemed now to be vibrating and shaking everywhere. Then it occurred to me there might be someone at the door. I opened it. The Fosters. The two Fosters.

They came in, obviously both talking at once, their mouths moving like fishes or birds, or cats after a meal – what an exercise of the jaws. I could not understand what they were saying. Their mouths became still. They were staring at me. It was my turn to move my mouth. I wondered if I should try to speak. I swallowed. I tried to remember my normal level of speech, and keeping the image in my mind I said, or I hoped that I said, —I've gone deaf, I've been to the doctor and there's nothing to be done, I'm deaf for life.

Not hearing my words, I felt cheated, as if I had been giving them away free. (*Just for something to say!*)

Elizabeth and Dorset stared hard at me, frowned, and then sat down on the sofa. Dorset began the eating motion which I now knew was the ejection of words or – speech.

Then he stopped speaking, and frowned with a facial, not a forehead, frown. Then he composed his face to its normal shape. His face and Elizabeth's face became suddenly generalised faces, those of people who are not deaf who are speaking to someone who is deaf. For life. The screens were down of course. I had put them up. They were adjusting them, securing them.

I reached for a sheet of paper and a pencil from the table behind me and wrote, —Yes, I'm deaf. There's nothing I can do about it.

I gave Dorset the paper and pencil. He gazed at the pencil in his hand as if it were a gun. He looked startled. *Have you never used a pencil before*, I said to myself, in the way I was soon to be conversing, to myself, without sound, and without eating the air around me.

—Have you seen a doctor? he wrote.

—Yes. For the rest of my stay here, I'm totally deaf.

—But won't you leave now? Go home? What will you do?

—I'll go home when my Fellowship's over. In the meantime I'll stay and get on with my work.

—But will you be able to work – *deaf*?

—Why not?

—But it's so strange, won't it be strange? Who will look after you?

This last remark was from Elizabeth.

—I'll look after myself of course, I wrote, trying to put my feeling of dignified and indignant independence into my words and not succeeding.

—It's terrible, Elizabeth wrote.

—Yes, it's awful, Dorset added. —If there's anything we can do –

—Not at the moment, thanks.

—You poor thing. Dorset had a friend who went blind. And my grandmother – Rose's grandmother too – was deaf, in her old age of course. Are you sure it's permanent?

—Yes. Permanent.

I'd long ago given up laughing at the joke of permanence ever since the Permanent Way which bisected our town was abandoned and overgrown with weeds and the wall of the old railway station collapsed, and the Inspector of the Permanent Way died.

—Are you *quite* sure? Isn't it too soon to know? What about specialists?

—I'm speaking the truth, I wrote, aware that the truth also was a joke.

Speaking the truth.

—Why don't you speak instead of writing, and we'll write. You speak.

Dorset crossed the last remark (Elizabeth's) out and wrote, —Can you speak?

Then he said something to Elizabeth and because I had not yet enough skill in lip-reading I tried to imagine what he had said. What would I have said, I wondered.

Confronted with the immediate personal, I supposed that I, too, would make a transformation to the distantly generalised, and look through a mist of fear, confusion, apprehension and sympathy, while the recognisable 'he' became the unfamiliar monstrous 'they'.

—They are often dumb as well as deaf.

—It often affects them mentally.

—They have to take care in the traffic.

They they they.

Elizabeth wrote, —Aren't there hearing aids you

can get? Would that help?

Feeling a satisfied completeness I wrote, —Nothing can help this kind of deafness.

—Why are you so sure? Dorset wrote. —You have to keep an open mind.

I wrote, —I'm sure. The doctor is sure.

—But he's only one out of many.

Then Dorset and Elizabeth put their heads close and it seemed to me they were whispering.

Dorset wrote, —You'd better speak. You might forget how to speak.

I watched him then. I watched his face. I could see his attitude as if it had a separate life. I saw it born, grow and set with the Dorset touch as soon as he recognised it. I sensed it was now immovable.

His attitude was, —You can hear if you want to. You can hear if you try. And remember to speak. Speak up. You have to fight what has overtaken you.

Dorset the school teacher, the old-style disciplinarian.

I looked at Elizabeth, trying to guess what she was thinking. I could swear that she was thinking, 'I wonder what Rose would have thought.'

After a time, when no one spoke and I felt myself once again sinking into an imprisoning loneliness,

Dorset wrote, —We have to go out to lunch. Will you be all right if we leave you?

I wrote, —Certainly. Please understand that I'll just go on with my work, everything as usual. Nothing has changed. Please understand. *Nothing has changed.*

I might easily have said, remembering the dead Inspector of the weedgrown Permanent Way, —All is Permanent. Let's sit down to the everlasting feast of the everlasting life. Even with music.

15

As I had expected, within the next two weeks, as the people I had met heard of my affliction they came out of curiosity and sympathy to visit me to offer advice, information and sympathy, all of which I took, I hope, with a good grace, for during those first few weeks I played the role of myself as a silent sufferer for whom, nevertheless, nothing had changed, as if in my love affair with life, although I had been betrayed, with life declaring itself unfaithful to me, I continued to affirm my love with the heaven-encircling lie which became a rainbow-circumstance of truth, *Nothing has changed*.

There was even a God in heaven who repeated the Beatitudes in skin-speech and eye-speech and naked-sole-of-the-foot-speech, *Blessed are they*.

Haniel and Louise Markham, the nearest in distance, their apartment only a few streets away, came the first week. I never learned how they knew of my deafness. They were not appalled by it, I found, as they might have been had I been stricken blind. They brought me books, a portable supply of words that I could only look at now, and see in my mind, for my inner hearing of them was fast vanishing and they were becoming to mean mouth-movements only, in others, and in myself mouth-and-throat movements. I turned the pages of the book of French poetry and *Du Côté de Chez Swann* and *La Littérature Anglaise par les Textes*, and I stared and stared at the words as if they were passersby whom I should never see again. How strange they looked!

> *As high as cypresses were wont to soar among the pliant wayfaring trees.*

That was Virgil, *Eclogue 1.25.*

> *It is a better and a wiser thing to be a starved apothecary than a starved poet; so back to the shop, Mr John, back to 'plasters, pills and ointment boxes'.*

That was *Blackwood's Magazine* writing of Keats'
Endymion.

> *And custom lie upon thee with a weight*
> *Heavy as frost, and deep almost as life!*

That was Wordsworth who shared the joke of me,
Harry Gill, with a character called, I believe, Goody
Blake. Harry Gill's physical makeup was not all it
should have been. Was it he whose legs swelled or was it
his teeth that chattered chattered chatter still?

> *He knows not, the man who dwells prosperously*
>   *on dry land,*
> *how careworn on the icy-cold ocean I have lived*
>   *through*
> *long winters, an exile from joy,*
> *cut off from kinsmen;*
> *encompassed with icicles.*

The old man, the Seafarer.

> *And every tongue, through utter drought,*
> *was withered at the root;*

That was the Ancient Mariner.

A spirit had followed them; one of the invisible inhabitants of this planet, neither departed souls nor angels.

My quotations do not reflect my own state of mind at the time – the Seafarer, the Ancient Mariner are themselves – how intensely they were! – though I felt in time the *tongue withered at the root* might apply to me.

—You will keep on with the scholarship, of course? Haniel wrote on the now ever-present sheet of note-paper.

—Yes.

—Rose Hurndell had her afflictions too, you know. She limped.

—Yes.

—She used a stick to walk.

—Yes.

I felt no jealousy or disdain at this comparison of afflictions. Even when one has reached the age of thirty-three one knows a little of the peculiarities shared by human beings, of the need to shine in sickness and in health: the biggest tumour, the biggest prize, the biggest strawberry in the garden, I am lame, ah but I am blind, my lameness almost cost me my life.

My blindness…

I hate like this…and this.

I love…like this…and this…

Even Hamlet, or should one say, Most of all, Hamlet, most human, put himself in the competitive field of brotherly love:

'I loved Ophelia. Forty thousand brothers…'

Match that if you will.

My wound had thirty stitches and I am alive to tell the tale.

—Will you be cured?

—No.

—Have you had the best advice?

—Yes.

This puzzled Haniel and Louise as it had Dorset and Elizabeth who, by the way, met Haniel and Louise at the front gate and conducted them to my front door, as if they had been pre-infected with my condition.

—Haniel is deaf in one ear.

—Oh.

—Haniel has a hearing aid.

—Oh.

As with the Fosters, conversation lapsed, even on paper, or especially on paper where the words had nothing to disguise their thinness and meanness, where an Oh became one disapproving syllable instead of an admiring incredulity; nor could the pen smile or gesture as it spoke, and though one would have expected the words to contain their own smiles they did not do so and the resulting silence instead of being enriched with the satisfactions of completed speech, vibrated with unhappiness and frustration; it was a barren plain; it was its own defoliant.

The Markhams, like the Fosters, suggested that I might need looking after: Louise reminded me that she had 'looked after' Rose Hurndell and there had been no complaints about her ability; after all, she was a trained nurse, and keeping Haniel alive, with his heart, kept her skill exercised.

All the same, I could tell that their main idea of salvation for me was books and more books, for they seemed to equate deafness with being housebound and in this they were not wholly incorrect for I was afraid to go into the street and I had not done so since my visit to

Dr Rumor and I had not protested when one morning Dorset and Elizabeth came to the door with their arms full of enough groceries to last at least two weeks.

Haniel and Louise promised to visit me regularly, each time bringing as many books as I asked for. It appeared that they were pleased to have me in what seemed to be permanent capture.

These seemings and appearings are necessary to my story, to counteract the material actualities among which were the refrigerator which continued to work, the oil-filled heater which continued to heat and the bandage-white hot water cylinder which continued to supply hot water.

—

I have to confess that my deafness alarmed and frightened me and I could not understand why the thought of taking some action or getting further advice paralysed me. Perhaps I was conducting a human experiment after all, living in prison, in a monastery, dyeing my senses a certain colour so as to fit a certain race whose prestige and welfare might have been more considered had it been blind. Whatever the reason, my deafness and my inability to take any action, if any could have been taken, persisted, and for two weeks I stayed in the small house receiving guests within a few days of each other, as the news spread, a process described by the local newspaper as *téléphone arabe*.

After the Markhams, I received in audience, as it were, George and Liz Lee who also brought books, *policiers*, in a plastic bag, as their belief appeared to be that my condition resembling convalescence, needed the traditional 'escape' literature. They seemed not to be aware of their betrayal of the literature which they had been trained to select and care for and dissemi-nate among the readers. I remembered with a feeling of horror the morning I had visited the English library and found the retired scholars from Oxford and Cambridge querulously picking over the much handled dog-eared green backed detective stories, and had seen the alarming hunger in their eyes as they found one they had not read; and had known that, for them, the *policiers* were more than casual holiday reading, they were an urgent transfusion for the perpetual state of convalescence which, whether or not they recognised it, their retirement had become or had always been. I'd heard two talking. Both were University Men. Both had a similar accent to George Lee although they were intelligible.

—I can't bear to look at Tolstoy, one had said.

—I can't look at any of them, the other replied. —Here, have you read this: *Campus Death?*

—*Campus Death?* I don't think so. Isn't he the author of *Death of a Don?*

—I think he is. A far cry from *The Death of Ivan Ilych*.

The other looked serious. —That kind of life's over for me, he said, with a wistfulness, as if he were talking of sex.

—I quite enjoy these detective stories. There's an art in them, you know. (He was defensive.)

—I find they're good to relax with.

What neither of them said was that when you plan to retire, to get to the country of perpetual relaxation, and you start travelling there and eventually arrive you may find you have picked up a perpetual sense of despair and a feeling of timelessness that is not merely the abandoning of timetables and not the grand eternity 'pinnacled dim in the intense inane', but a prospect of desert, of fruitlessness from which death begins to appear, enticingly, as the last springtime.

—You'll feel better reading these, George Lee prescribed as he spilled the books from their plastic bag on to the sofa beside me. I caught a glimpse of lurid covers, bloodied wounds and daggers, corpses, cloaks, heavy furniture, bureaux, bare-shouldered women laughing, dead.

—They look ghastly, but you'll relax with these.

—Aren't you betraying all those 'other' books in your library? I wrote.

Liz was cheerful. I could tell by her smile and her quick gestures.

—Not at all. A detective novel is good for you.

For most of their visit we sat in the usual silence. The palm trees outside were waving furiously in what appeared to be a very strong wind indeed. The air was hot, stinging with the feel of sand even in the room.

—The wind is blowing from the Sahara, Liz wrote. —Is this your first sirocco?

My natural shyness came over me. I was aware of the vulnerability that accompanies 'first' experiences. I thought of the created world within its first week of creation and the raging sensitivity of every material manifestation – the first time of light, of dark, night, day of dust leaves, creatures – a trembling enough time; but for man, who has memory, perhaps a time for which, in the experience of the explosion of his senses, he still pays, for which the darkening rather than the illumination of memory is acclaimed as a blessed state.

The creation of the world. A great distance from my first sirocco. I had to rely, now, entirely on my sight and my imagination, my sense of touch, smell and space, for my appreciation of the sirocco.

In my mind I half-heard a theatrical wind and I saw, suddenly, a book from which I had learned to read, with a page called 'The Wind' and the picture of the people in the streets, the hats held, skirts billowing, sunshades turned inside out, trees and flowers bowed to earth, a man chasing his bowler hat along the street, dogs running. I saw in my mind, then, a 'literary' wind. A literal wind, literarily portrayed.

In actuality, here, from the window of the small house, I watched with George and Liz Lee the sirocco swirl upon the town. The agitation of the palms was terrible to see. The sky became filled with clouds billowing with an orange tint like the smoke of a distant fire: it was a colour that seen in the sky has the power to fill the heart with foreboding; it was an 'earthquake colour', the colour of an ancient battlefield in the time of huge cannons operated by men diminished in comparison, and it was also the colour of a hydrogen bomb, an atom operated by men so tall in comparison that their shadow could take a twilight walk from horizon to horizon across the earth.

—Three years ago, George wrote on a new sheet of paper, —houses near the promenade were flattened.

I did not write an answer but I looked impressed. I was also amused, as I thought suddenly that my deafness was not such a calamity if it could eliminate from conversation the curious custom of the you-are-about-to-be-amazed question followed by the now-this-will-amaze-you answer.

—No.

A 'no' that lies between these two amazements is one of the hardest words to pronounce.

—You don't know what happened?

—No.

—Houses near the promenade were flattened!

I did feel relieved that through my deafness I was escaping the heavy conversationalists who make one work for the privilege of speaking to them, whose every remark demands a visible explosive response.

Also, I was escaping George's 'Angela will be livid.

Old, retired.'

—Can you go out in the sirocco? I wrote.

—Oh yes, this isn't so bad. We must be leaving you.

As Liz wrote she spoke the words, or moved her lips in an exaggerated manner.

—You will have to learn to lip-read. And you mustn't give up speaking.

I think I said, —No, I shan't give up speaking.

As I spoke I put my hand on my throat, taking my voice by the hand, as it were, to encourage it. I felt its vibrations but of course I heard nothing.

—There's the deaf and dumb language, the finger language, too, George wrote.

Then both looked at me. Their faces were full of sympathy.

—It's worse away from your native land, George wrote.

I had the feeling he was referring to himself and not to me.

~

My next visitors, again after an interval of a few days, were Connie and Max Watercress.

—We've heard, Connie wrote when I gave her the sheet of paper and a pen.

Reading what she had written, she blushed beneath her layer of makeup for she had a sensitivity which operated apart from herself and which she did not recognise: she and it were strangers living in the same house; a curious position to be in; the effect was that of startling her every now and again with her own feelings and intuitions.

She crossed out what she had written, adding, —We're terribly sorry. What an extraordinary thing to have happened. Is it really permanent?

I wrote, —Yes. Permanent.

She frowned and said something to Max who looked at me closely, that is to say, he inspected me with his large swimmingly brown eyes behind their magnified lenses.

—What about the Fellowship? he wrote.

—What about it?

—We can't have it harmed in any way.

—What do you mean, 'harmed'?

Both Connie and Max looked uncomfortable upon reading my question.

—Are you sure you wouldn't rather that someone

else came to take up the Fellowship?

Hesitating a moment, Connie wrote, —Someone younger?

—But I'm thirty-three!

—Of course, of course. But it's perhaps a bad age.

—What do you mean, a bad age?

—Well, in between. We could ask someone younger to step in…to help you of course, for you can't stay in Menton, can you?

—Why not?

—Not deaf, surely?

—Why not?

—We're only thinking of your own welfare.

Max underlined this last sentence.

Connie took the pen from Max and wrote, —You'll miss so much of the life, so many experiences through being deaf. You won't be using the Fellowship to good advantage.

I was obstinate.

—I'll be using it as much as I can. And it's *my* Fellowship. It may be the Watercress-Armstrong Fellowship in honour of Rose Hurndell bless her thorns and blossoms and haemorrhaged brain but it's been awarded to me and I don't see how my being deaf or dumb or blind can affect it.

—Don't be angry, Harry. Of course, the Committee awarded you the Fellowship but we have to think of the Fellowship, you know.

—You mean if I had been deaf when I applied I might not have been awarded it?

—We have to have people who can cope.

—I can cope.

—You can cope less now than you could with your hearing. You might have a traffic accident. You won't be able to speak to people. You can't spend all your time in correspondence.

—Why not? Have you anyone in mind to take over the Fellowship?

Max and Connie looked at each other and did not try to write their answer. I wrote it for them.

—What about Michael? He's getting a reputation as a writer. He's written some good stories.

Immediately they became parents rather than guardians of a Fellowship. Forgetting for the moment that I was deaf, Connie looked at Max and said (I knew by heart what she would say and my study of her lips showed me my surmise was correct), —He's such a clever boy.

I found myself mimicking her within myself.

—*Such a clever boy.*
—*He has perfect pitch.*
—*Perfect pitch.*
—*He could be anything.*

Clever boy, perfect pitch, beard, he could be anything.
I wrote on my paper, —What about his beard?
Connie looked puzzled.
—What do you mean?
—He is perfect for the part.
She looked relieved.
—Do you think so?
—Yes.
—You suggest then that you give up the Fellowship,
we fly you home to New Zealand for expert medical
treatment, and we give the Fellowship to Michael –
after a committee meeting of course, with a decision
made unanimously by the Committee?

I hope that I looked coldly at her and I cursed ball-
point pens or any kind of pen that cannot also convey
cold looks.

I wrote, —I suggest no such thing. I was awarded

the Fellowship and I'm keeping it, deaf or dumb or blind or mad or whatever.

—Even if you can't cope?

—Who said I can't cope?

—You're deaf. Some harm may come to the Fellowship.

As I read her words I realised that she and Max looked on the Fellowship as a live creature which they had hatched together and which they felt they had to protect. Their possessive instinct was fierce. I sensed that there might be for them times when even Rose Hurndell, dead, for whom the Fellowship was a memorial, could be a danger, perhaps as much a danger as the living writers who did not play the game of, as it were, fitting the garment that had been cut and sewn for them, particularly when they learned how closely it resembled a shroud!

—But we've never had a deaf Fellow.

—You have one now.

—The Committee will have to look into it.

I was angry.

—Let the Committee look into it. I'm staying.

Suddenly their attitude changed. They became sympathetic.

—Of course you can stay. You *are* the Fellow. We were just thinking of your own welfare and what you will do now that you're deaf.

They made the same remark as the Lees.

—You can't give up speaking just because you're deaf. You might become deaf-and-dumb.

Their writing deaf-and-dumb in hyphens frightened me; I don't recall being frightened before by hyphens. These told me that I now had an inevitable label, that I was parcelled, tied in string with 'deaf' and 'dumb' as the two ends of the bow – bows can be undone – no, it was more than that – I had been made my own complement, sealed by the hyphens to words whose function is to seal – deaf-and-dumb, over-and-under, up-and-down, back-and-forth, black-and-white, cash-and-carry, pen-and-ink, words which, because they range in two hemispheres of meaning, have a deceptive sense of space and freedom until one is trapped within them by the boundary-making mouths of beings who talk, meaning no harm.

He's deaf-and-dumb.

I was.

I was even afraid now to put my hand to my throat to feel the vibrations of my voice – at least I hesitated to do this, in company. I could not quite believe that I had been silenced perhaps for life by the fact that one word not being entirely at home on its own, tended to ally itself to another. Deaf-and-dumb. Not deaf-and-happy, deaf-and-peaceful, deaf-and-industrious.

I was not dumb.

—I'm not dumb, I said, or hoped that I said.

Connie and Max looked startled. Obviously I had spoken too loud.

—He's shouting, Connie said.

I read her lips.

—He doesn't know he's shouting, Max answered.

The feeling of loneliness came over me once more as I watched the lips moving with the recognisable words, the words utterly isolated from sound expression – I had not realised until then that we own the words we speak as we own the food we swallow or reject; we own the words, command them, shift them, re-emphasise them; they, powerful, have little power over our speaking them; the loneliness that came over me was caused, I think, by the degradation of the words, their descent from the pampered sheltered ones to the homeless outcasts that could not be spared an inflexion or a morsel of emphasis or a loving hesitation.

I'll shout if I like, I thought.

—So you see I'm not dumb.

Connie took the paper and wrote, —We know you're not dumb. Your voice is too loud. Did you know? We must go now. We hope your deafness doesn't interfere with your writing.

Max took the paper then, and wrote, —We hope you'll think seriously about your condition. Medicine is always dearer in another country.

I wrote in reply, —Everything is always comparative in another country. Crooks are crookeder, grass is greener, heights are higher, words are wordier, pleasures are more pleasurable, death is deader, life is livelier, dogs are doggier, fortune is more fortunate, vaults more vaulted, distance is further, water more watery, blue is bluer, grey is greyer, fame more famous, continuance more continuing, consumers more consumed, reality more real, fantasy more fantastic, adjustments more adjusted, fires more fiery, chaos more chaotic…I mean to say…

(Both Connie and Max were beginning to look impatient at my cataloguing.)

—I also mean to say, the deaf are deafer and the dumb are dumber. Is that not so?

—You mustn't be bitter, Connie wrote. Remember you're the Watercress-Armstrong Fellow.

I smiled as I shook hands with them, in the French way, as I saw them out the front door.

Remember you're the Watercress-Armstrong Fellow.

How will I forget it? I thought, wishing I would let myself speak, shouting or no shouting but I did not want the hyacinths, just breaking into bud by the door, to curdle and curl their blue petals all for the sake of a human voice that from now on had to go out of my mouth alone, without any guidance, and which in its confusion might give the impression of rage or hate, any emotion, all in a frightening incongruity enough to scare the words back into my mouth.

I did not want to see a scarred or burned track like a no man's land wherever my spoken words passed by; I did not want to destroy the ordinary vegetation of ordinary conversation, the desultory communication that accomplishes its dull purpose of communicating without undue melodrama or tragedy or even comedy.

I did not want my words to be, unknown to me, missiles, sticks and stones.

I knew that I had not felt, before, this tenderness towards words. Somehow I had always thought they could look after themselves, they could be used and even abused and they would always recover or sleep it off within the pages of the dictionary where most of them spent most of their time anyway. I suppose it will affect my writing, I thought. My being deaf. Deaf-and-dumb. And all these words with no sound to them and even their inner sound doomed to a gradual diminishing. The musical notes, at least, can look after themselves, they're nonentities, slabs of vanilla, spaghetti, it is *they* who are the sticks and stones, they have no reliance on the human mouth and the human ear; we eavesdrop on words; music eavesdrops on our ears.

Eavesdrop.

What a dew filled word it sounded, *sounded* in my still inviolate inner ear. Eavesdrop.

In a world of lost eaves. Eaves had scarcely been my word at all. My word was 'gutter', 'spouting'. The word 'eaves' was at peace in a literary world.

I eavesdropped.

I overheard. I underheard.

I think that as Connie and Max Watercress went out the gate they called out to me, —Michael and Grace are coming to see you in a couple of days.

I did not hear them. Nor did I read their lips. I knew

what they said, my knowing a combination of intuition, common sense and a grasp of the momentary intersection of circumstance and people and an imagination of the signposts which the people carried or remarked in their minds. I was to learn to use this intuition with increasing skill that often led others to suppose that I was not always deaf or completely deaf, that I could 'switch on or off' at will. This idea of the deaf hearing only what they want to hear is a neat explanation which survives as clichés and commonplaces do, by its neatness and apparent unassailability. It is wishful thinking, the longing to reclaim the power of mind over body particularly when an overwhelming illness or disability has washed in like an eroding tide over the shores of the body. In my deafness I could not hear what I thought that I wanted to hear. I could hear nothing.

Constantly I was aware also that by being deaf and not blind I was being deprived of some romantic fulfilment of a finer tragedy. The comparison between deafness and blindness occupied those who knew me. There would be long debates on whether it was 'better' to be deaf or blind, always with the assumption that one affliction was necessary. The first remark of many people meeting me for the first time and knowing of my deafness was:

—It's better than being blind, anyway.

—I suppose you're glad you're not blind.

Then would follow, if two or more people had come to 'cheer me up' or for whatever other reason, the discussion about which *they'd* rather be. It was a game they played, like the child's game of choosing between two offered treats, both equally enticing – a golden ring or a silver casket, a castle or a farm with two hundred head of cattle; or even marriage partners – a princess or a scullery maid. At times their discussion became so clinical that it reminded me of a conference of insurance agents meeting to put a price on lost eyes and hearing and other facilities and pleasures and limbs; fortunately I remained unpriced.

~

I was still 'at home', after three weeks of deafness, when the final visitors (among those connected in some way with the Fellowship and Rose Hurndell) arrived: Michael and Grace Watercress.

Michael looked afraid and diffident. It was Grace

who opened the conversation, —Is there anything you need?

—No thanks. What are you doing these days?

I could see that Michael was relieved to take his mind from my deafness, yet it was not he who answered.

—He's working on a novel.

I felt pangs of jealousy. Take over the Fellowship? Why shouldn't he? He'd already been an understudy and even moved into the role. His appearance was so much his ally. The easily identifiable writer; whereas I had long experience of being ignored because I resembled a clerk, a doctor, a commercial traveller, anything but the accepted idea of a 'writer'. I wondered then at the feelings of an understudy who never takes over the major role at the last minute.

I wrote, —Congratulations. Some day he'll be applying for the Watercress-Armstrong Fellowship.

—Sooner than you think, Grace wrote, glancing proudly at Michael.

What a paragon of a writer he was! I simply couldn't deny it. If I'd had any of my books with me I could have walked to the bookshelf and opened any volume with photos of writers and found Michael Watercress among the great Russians, the Americans, the French, the

English; he was international. His eyes and face were intelligent as far as liveliness can be equated with intelligence, and although I did feel a sneaking jealousy of his ability to play the role in costume of a writer I felt that perhaps (in spite of his wife's and his parents' repeated reference to the 'the young Hemingway') his talent did not match his appearance. I was pre-judging, not having read his work, but I felt that he lacked the singleness of purpose necessary. His thoughts and the thoughts of others were constantly on what he would achieve, on what he would become, in a pleasantly anticipated future, while the present lay just at hand, all the riches in the world ignored and untouched. It was scarcely Michael's fault. I could see that his clever childhood had been a grooming, an anticipation, for the future use of his many talents, and he had fallen into the habit of tomorrow which in a man of thirty-three shows a rosy promise beginning to wither and arouses pity rather than admiration. Poor chap, I thought. He's already going to seed. Destroyed by his promising future. A man without a past or present. Was he not then a completely unmetaphorical man, deprived of time?

~

Now that I was deaf, I was becoming more used to interior monologues, of the type that had always bored me when I tried to read fiction. Within the past few weeks, however, I had been so shocked at the banality of my paper conversations that I almost resolved to give them up; I'd come across pages and pages of seeming 'manuscript' only to find them covered with:

—We hope you're feeling better.

—I am thank you.

—Are you sure you're permanently deaf?

—Oh yes.

—You must not forget how to speak. Speak.

—Speak Philip Sparrow, Speke!

—What do you mean?

—It's a quotation.

—I see. Anyway it's better than being blind or crippled.

—How do you know?

—It must be, surely.

—How do you know?

—Surely.

—Surely what?

—It's better to be deaf than blind.

—Why?

—You're less dependent for one thing. You can walk around on your own. Though you can't hear the traffic. Can you hear the traffic?

—No.

—Not at all?

—No.

—You want to be careful then. The driving's reckless. It's a foreign country, remember.

—Oh yes. A foreign country. The dead are deader, the grass is greener, etc. and the reckless are more reckless.

—You will be careful, won't you?

—Yes yes.

—I am so glad you're not blind or crippled.

~

Always, you see, they had the last word. It amused me, in my interior monologues, to suppose what the last word might be. And what, indeed, was the first word?

~

Yours truly

Yours very truly

Yours affectionately

Faithfully yours

Cordially yours

Respectfully yours

Yours sincerely

Yours lovingly

Yours gratefully

Lovingly yours

I remain

I remain

Never use ruled paper for any correspondence

never use tinted paper for business letters

do not use simplified spelling

never use dear friend, friend Jack, my dear friend or fiend

Bliss

never use oblige in the place of a complimentary close

always write yours sincerely

never write a letter in the heat of anger

do not attempt to put anything on paper without first thinking it out and arranging what you want to say

We beg to state

we beg to advise

answering yours of the 21st inst. order has been delayed but will ship goods at once

please send a remittance by return mail

if we can be of use to you in the future will you let us know

please investigate the delay at once

On Tuesday June the fourteenth Mr Smith and I are to be married. The ceremony will be at home and we are asking a few close friends. I hope you will be able to come. Owing to the death of my father we are to be married at home. We shall be delighted to attend your wedding. Unfortunately our ship is sailing that day and we cannot attend.

Will you please give us the pleasure of your company at a small dinner on Thursday. I hope you are not other-wise engaged that evening. We regret that we cannot accept your kind invitation but unfortunately we have a previous engagement.

I am giving a little dinner party and one of my guests has just told me he cannot be present on account of a sudden death. Will you kindly help out. It is indeed fortunate for me that Harry Talbot cannot be present. Thank you for thinking of me.

Will you come to luncheon tomorrow?

—

It is with the deepest sympathy that I learned of your bereavement. Please accept our heartfelt sympathy. I am sorely grieved to learn of the death of your husband. I am grateful for your comforting letter. Thank you for your sympathy. Do not measure our appreciation by the length of time it has taken us to reply. I knew that you would be sorry for us. Congratulations on your birthday. I am sending you a little gift as a token of appreciation for your kindness to me. Please accept my heartiest good wishes on this, the fifteenth anniversary of your marriage. Congratulations on the birth of your daughter. The bearer of this note is an old friend of mine. He knows nobody in Little Gidding and anything you can do to make his stay pleasant I shall greatly appreciate. This will introduce you to Clara Wells. She is a girl of charming personality and has many accomplishments. Your handsome Christmas gift is something I have wanted for a long time. I very much appreciate the exquisite flowers which you so kindly sent to Mrs Dee. She is rapidly improving and will soon be about again. You were very kind to entertain my cousin. I am so glad you have recovered from your recent illness. Please send as soon as possible to my charge account the following goods 1 dozen towels 2 pairs brown leather shoes three pairs of curtains for casement windows 6ft high and ten feet wide. I have your inquiry concerning my former gardener. I hope that you don't think me discourteous but I prefer not to discuss him. This is to certify that Montgomery Hellman has been in my employ for five years. He is sober, honest and I have always found him thoroughly dependable. Will you let me know as soon as possible if you have any four-roomed houses in the neighbourhood. About two acres of ground, with lawn and vegetable and flower garden? I have just had my son's report for the term. I notice he did not pass in mathematics. This leads me to believe that perhaps he is spending too much time on other matters. What is your opinion? I enclose my cheque for 100 pounds for the silver candlesticks. Our spring sales are being held this week. Will you be there? Have you ever counted the cost of making your pickles jams and jellies at home? In a couple of weeks you are going to think a good deal about your new overcoat. Why not start thinking now? Would you like us to dispose of your property for you? We have attractive styles in pocket cheque books that might interest you. May I call your attention to the question which every man of property must at some time gravely consider and that is the disposition of your estate after your death. Please send me as soon as possible 3 pairs ribbed stockings size nine. I regret to inform you that the dishwasher has failed to live up to your guarantee. We are sorry to learn that you found two buttons missing from your suit. We cannot have your teaspoons monogrammed as you wish. Our letters of March 9, April 19th, have brought no reply from you. You naturally wish to keep your credit clear. We wish to have it clear. Will you not send a cheque and keep the account on a pleasant basis? We have no desire to resort to the law to collect the hundred pounds owing by you unless the remittance is in our hands we shall take definite steps for the legal collection of your account. May we hear from you at once?

I can take dictation at the rate of a hundred words a minute. I am willing to work. Will you let me try? I am looking for a position as a cashier. This is to certify that Mabel Howard has been in my employ for fifteen months. She is a most willing and able worker. Merry Christmas to you and all the family. May each of the three hundred and sixty-five days of the new year be a happy one for you. May your Easter be a bright and happy one. Birthday greetings. You have our heartfelt sympathy. Heartiest congratulations. Thank you for your courteous letter in reply to my application in your department. I am especially desirous of becoming associated with your house.

May you have the strength to bear this great affliction. Our love and sympathy. I have heard a rumour of your sad news. Many people have gone through this experience. Many people recover. Your own courage and cheerfulness are your best medicine. Would you like letters from me?